DEADLY HUNTER

A pair of glittering amber eyes set in a face of long white fur stared back at her. Its jaws were open. She glimpsed white fangs — so close...

Bethan screamed, lost her balance and slithered down the slope.

Laura couldn't move.

Couldn't breathe.

But suddenly she knew how a small animal would feel just before falling prey to some hungry beast.

Because she was the prey.

And this massive white wolf was the predator.

HIPPO MYSTERY

DEADLY HUNTER

Ann Evans

Hippo

Scholastic Children's Books,
Commonwealth House, 1–19 New Oxford Street,
London, WC1A 1NU, UK
a division of Scholastic Ltd
London ~ New York ~ Toronto ~ Sydney ~ Auckland

First published by Scholastic Ltd., 1998

Text copyright © Ann Evans, 1998

ISBN 0 590 19716 9

Typeset by TW Typesetting, Midsomer Norton, Somerset
Printed by Caledonian International Book Manufacturing Ltd,
Glasgow

10 9 8 7 6 5 4 3 2 1

For Debbie and Gary

Chapter 1

"It was a nightmare," Gary wailed, throwing his school bag under his desk and slumping down into his chair. "That bloke cared more about his rotten car than hitting my dog!"

Laura pulled off her gloves and woolly hat so that a mop of black curls exploded around her face. "Poor Kess. People can be so cruel."

"I can still see his big ugly face," Gary said, his brown eyes glittering angrily. "Said it was my fault for not having her on a lead. But Kess never needs a lead."

"I know," Laura murmured, perching herself on the corner of his desk by the classroom window. "She's a brilliant dog."

Gary's shoulders slumped miserably. "Maybe I should have put her on a lead. There's no pavement that part of Coopers Lane. Only he was driving like a maniac. He must have seen us. He could have given Kess a bit more room… Poor old girl."

Laura gazed sadly through the classroom window. A light flutter of snowflakes was beginning to fall. Last winter when it had snowed, they'd all gone sledging up on Badger Hill. Kess too. Bounding through snowdrifts. Barking that distinctive high-pitched collie bark of hers.

A lump rose in her throat. "Kess will be all right, won't she?"

Gary blinked rapidly, determined to keep the tears at bay. "Yeah! She's a tough old thing."

"Did the driver help get Kess to the vet's?"

Gary shook his head. "You've got to be joking. He just looked down his nose at Kess lying in the road, then examined his car for dents. He didn't even say sorry or stroke her or anything." His eyes blazed with anger. "If I ever see him again, he's gonna be sorry. He'll pay for it."

Laura was horrified. "He didn't try to help you? That's awful."

"He just sneered, got into his car and drove off," said Gary unhappily.

"Oh, that's terrible," Laura murmured.

"What's terrible?" Bethan asked, dropping her school bag on a chair and deliberately shaking snowflakes all over Laura and Gary.

"Thanks!" said Laura, brushing them off.

"My pleasure," she grinned, taking her coat off and pushing her long fair hair back from her face. "So, what's up?"

Laura glanced at Gary, then softly said, "It's Kess. She was hit by a car last night."

Bethan's face crumpled. "Oh no, not Kess! That's awful. How is she?"

"Broken leg and internal injuries," Gary answered stiffly. "It's the internal injuries that are the worst. If we'd got her to the vet's quicker... If that bloke had helped instead of just driving off..." His hands clenched into fists. "If I ever get my hands on him, I'll make him regret not helping us..."

Miss Clark, their teacher, came in then and everyone shuffled into their places.

"Good news!" the teacher exclaimed, after calling the register. "Those of you doing your winter project on the Media will be visiting our local radio station, FM Classic Discs, next Wednesday."

A hubbub of delighted chatter sprang up.

"Quietly now!" said Miss Clark. "Also, for the small group who are doing their project on endangered species – that's Laura, Bethan and Gary, yes?"

"Yes, miss," the two girls answered.

"I've organized for you to go behind the scenes, so to speak, at Cottesbrook Rare Breeds Park."

Laura beamed at Bethan and Gary. But Gary was staring broodily out of the window.

"When, miss?" Bethan asked eagerly.

"This Saturday morning, eleven o'clock. Colonel Cartwright-Holmes who owns and runs the park is expecting you. It's actually only open to the public at weekends this time of year. So you're very fortunate that he's giving you some of his valuable time to show you around and talk to you. Now make sure you've prepared your questions thoroughly –

and be polite!"

Laura hoped the trip would cheer Gary up a bit. But he spent the day moping and looking at his watch.

As soon as the final bell went, he was off, not bothering to wait for them, his sad face hidden under his hood and scarf.

Laura pushed her hands deep into her pockets as she and Bethan walked home. "Poor Gary, he's really upset about Kess."

"It's not good, is it," agreed Bethan. "And fancy that bloke not helping. Honestly, some people!"

"Not everyone's an animal lover," Laura remarked. "At least Kess is being well looked after now. We'll just have to hope and pray."

They walked briskly, the frost cold on their faces. Living as they did on the outskirts of the small country town, school was just a fifteen minute walk from home. And while it was just a bus ride into the heart of the town for major shopping excursions, they had their own little community of shops and amenities practically on the doorstep.

And best of all, not minutes from the streets

where they lived, were the wild open moors that stretched for as far as the eye could see.

"Should be good on Saturday," Bethan remarked cheerfully. "Our own personal look behind the scenes."

"It's brilliant," Laura agreed. "You know, we could take a walk down there tomorrow after school as well. It's only about a mile out of town. We could take some photographs of the park from the outside. Landscape shots, things like that."

Bethan grinned. "You just can't wait to take some practice piccies with your new action-packed, zoom lens, 35 millimetre posh birthday camera – which you're dying to try out!"

Laura laughed. "That's the one. Only it's not posh. It's second hand. My uncle Eddie got himself a new one and gave me his old one for my birthday."

"It looked posh when I saw it," Bethan said breezily.

"It's ancient!" exclaimed Laura. "And all I've got to do now is figure out how to use it!"

* * *

By Friday afternoon, Laura had read and re-read the camera's instruction booklet. And she'd rung her uncle to double check how to work the light meter and alter the settings.

"I'm off now, mum," she called, peeping round the sitting room door. The warm scent of talcum powder and baby lotion wafted out.

Her mother glanced up from changing her baby brother's nappy. "Make sure you're back before dark."

"Will do."

"And you're meeting Bethan and Gary?"

"Meeting Bethan, calling for Gary."

"So long as you're not alone. Cottesbrook Park is awfully isolated, specially with the woods right next to it."

"We'll be OK, Mum."

Her mother frowned. "You know, it's going to take you a good twenty minutes to walk there."

"We'll be back before it's dark, promise. Don't worry."

Laura set off towards Bethan's house in the next street. Being alone or isolated never worried her. Their house was the very last house in the street. And their street led directly out on to the moors with nothing but wild open countryside and distant forests for as far as the eye could see.

Now the usual greens and browns of the moors were dusted with a powdery-white snow. And as it shifted and gusted in the wind, it looked as if the entire moorland was shimmering.

Turning away, she pulled her collar up, hitched her camera bag on to her shoulder and set off towards Bethan's house.

Her friend met her halfway. "Look at you!" she teased. "You look like a real photo-grapher!"

"One day," Laura said wistfully. "A photo-journalist – that's what I'm going to be. Going to war-torn countries, reporting on the plight of the people."

"And I'll be mending all their broken bones when I'm a top surgeon," said Bethan. "Talking of which, I wonder how Kess is."

"We'll soon know," Laura said, as they reached Gary's house.

His mother answered the door. "Sorry girls,

Gary's at the vet's. They let him sit with Kess for as long as he wants. They're awfully kind."

"How is she?" asked Laura.

"It doesn't look good. If only she'd been operated on sooner…" She sighed. "Gary is so worried."

"I'm sure she'll be all right," Laura said encouragingly.

"Let's hope so," Gary's mum agreed, looking anything but hopeful. "Oh I nearly forgot, Gary mentioned something about going to the rare breeds park tomorrow. Or rather, *not* going."

Laura groaned. "Oh he must come. We need him."

"He just wants to be with Kess," she sighed. "But I'll try and persuade him. It'll take his mind off things for a while."

Laura glanced at Bethan as they headed down Coopers Lane which took them out into the countryside, towards the rare breeds park. "Looks like it could be just you and me tomorrow. Ah well, let's get going while it's still light enough to take some photos."

Bethan raised her eyebrows. "I bet you haven't even got a film in it!"

Chapter 2

Two stone eagles sat on tall pillars at the entrance to Cottesbrook Rare Breeds Park. The wrought iron gates were padlocked and a high brick wall encircled the front of the park and the adjoining house – home, the girls guessed, to Colonel Cartwright-Holmes.

To the right of the entrance, where the wall curved around to encompass the park, a forest of pines, oaks and elm trees grew up, stretching far into the distance.

"My wide-angled lens, I think," Laura mused, placing her camera bag on the ground and stooping down to delve through its now familiar contents.

A narrow country lane ran in front of the

park and forest, but there was little traffic, and Laura took a few shots of the view untroubled by passing vehicles.

"Now what?" Bethan mused.

Laura wrinkled her nose. "I know! If we walk along by the wall, we'll reach the part where there's just wire fencing. I remember years ago when my dad took me to see the animals, you could see the forest from inside the park. So it can't be all brick wall, can it?"

Bethan's blue eyes widened. "You want to go *in* the forest? I thought I was the scatty one!"

"Yes, why not? Oh, come on. We can take some more landscape shots," Laura said, grabbing her arm. "We won't go far and we'll keep to the edge. Come on, we won't get lost or anything."

Bethan narrowed her eyes. "Now why does that sound like someone's famous last words?"

Laura laughed. "Come on!"

"OK, OK, I'm coming."

They crossed the quiet lane and peered through the wrought iron gates before heading into the forest. There was a long driveway which was blockaded off by a tall wooden partition, equipped with turnstiles and a ticket kiosk. To the left was another fence with an arched gateway leading to the front entrance of the sprawling country house.

"Hope we don't have to pay tomorrow," Bethan remarked as they walked on, skirting the brick wall that stretched deep into the forest.

"Me too," Laura agreed, shivering suddenly as the shadow of the trees made everything colder. And although protected from the wind by the trees, they were made more aware of it as it howled and whistled and sighed through the bare branches.

They walked in single file along a narrow dirt track, brick wall to the left, forest to their right. And underfoot a thick mulch of fallen leaves and bracken crackled and squelched as they picked their way along by the park's perimeter wall.

"How much further?" Bethan groaned as the wall stretched on and on, endlessly.

"Not sure, but if we don't find the wire bit in a minute we'd better go back. We've come further than I intended already."

Then suddenly Laura spotted the landscape opening up ahead of them. The wall ended abruptly and a tall inter-linking wire fence took over, curved inwards at the top and edged with curls of razor wire.

"There! I knew it!" Laura exclaimed, dashing on ahead, and clambering up a steep muddy embankment to peer through the fencing. Cottesbrook Rare Breeds Park stretched out beyond.

She stood pressed up against the fence, which curled round in a giant arc, encompassing the patchwork of animal enclosures and cages and aviaries and reptile houses. A herd of deer was grazing far off in the distance, in another fenced-off enclosure white foxes trotted back and forth, and in another, strange fawn and black dog-like animals were playing on the grassy slopes of a mound of earth at the centre of their enclosure.

"Beth, come up!" Laura called. "You can see everything from up here."

Bethan scrambled up the slope, hanging on to the fence to stop herself slipping backwards. "These are new boots, you know."

14

"They'll clean," Laura replied with a grin. "Just look, Beth. Look at that view. Isn't it great?"

"Wonderful," Bethan agreed, rubbing her boot on some grass.

"Wide-angled lens again, I think," Laura said, stooping down and unzipping her camera case.

"Hello, what's going on down there?" Bethan asked suddenly.

Laura glanced through the fencing. Way across the park a lorry was bumping its way slowly between the animal enclosures, followed by two men on foot. It stopped at one of the enclosures. A man in a sheepskin jacket unlocked its gates, while the other – a dark-skinned man – threw chunks of meat into the far corner of the enclosure.

The pack of strange-looking dogs, with the pointed ears and white-tipped tails, descended on the meat ravenously.

"Feeding time at the zoo," Laura remarked, looking down her lens and getting the scene into focus.

"Hey!" Bethan exclaimed. "The lorry's

going into the enclosure where the dog-things are. That's odd."

As they watched through the perimeter fence, they saw the darker man close the gates behind them and follow the lorry to the grassy mound at the centre of the animal enclosure.

Laura quickly switched lenses, screwing into place the long zoom lens that brought everything up close.

Bethan glanced at her. "Know what you're doing, do you?"

"I think so," Laura replied confidently.

"Take the lens cap off then."

"I was just going to!"

Bethan peered through the netting. "They're heading straight towards that funny little hill. Oh wow! Look at that!"

To their amazement, the men opened two doors in the grassy mound, throwing them wide so that a square black hole appeared out of nowhere.

"It's not a real hill!" Bethan gasped.

"It must be one of those underground bunkers they used in the war," Laura said, twisting the lens so that everything came into focus. "I remember my grandad telling me about them."

"Take some photos," Bethan urged.

"I am," Laura murmured, clicking away as the lorry driver walked into the bunker and returned driving a fork-lift truck. A moment later they began unloading big wooden crates from the lorry and storing them in the bunker.

Within minutes the job was done, the bunker doors were closed and it was simply a grassy mound again. Men and lorry were gone.

No one would ever have known it had happened.

"Must be their store room," Bethan suggested. "Now that's what I call being environmentally friendly!"

Laura's eyes sparkled. "This project of ours is going to be brilliant!"

She crouched down close to the perimeter fencing to pack away her camera equipment. Chatting to Bethan as to how they could best display their project work, neither of them heard the deadly silent padding of large paws stealing towards them.

They didn't see the lithe muscular body moving stealthily nearer, nor the keen amber eyes fixed upon them.

Not until the huge white animal was within a centimetre of Laura's face, and she felt its breath hot on her cheek, did she sense danger.

Then her skin prickled.

She raised her eyes slowly, almost afraid to look...

A pair of glittering amber eyes set in a face of long white fur stared back at her. Its jaws were open. She glimpsed white fangs – so close...

Bethan screamed, lost her balance and slithered down the slope.

Laura couldn't move.

Couldn't breathe.

But suddenly she knew how a small animal would feel just before falling prey to some hungry beast.

Because she was the prey.

And this massive white wolf was the predator.

It drew back its black lips, revealing two rows of large sharp fangs. Its snarl was low, almost silent. Menacing.

A deadly, terrifying sound.

Chapter 3

Laura staggered backwards, her heart thudding, thankful for the high fences and walls. If that wolf was to escape...

"Take its picture," Bethan called, scrambling to her feet but keeping well away from the fence – and the wolf on the other side of it.

But Laura was shaking. The fencing was all that separated the wolf from them. It seemed little protection somehow. She had never been so close to a wolf before. And never seen one quite so magnificent.

A mixture of awe and fear made her hands tremble as she raised the camera to her eye. But before she could take its picture, the wolf turned tail and loped off.

"Where did it go?" Bethan gasped, scrambling back up the slope.

Laura peered along the wire perimeter, puzzled. There was no sign of it. "I don't know ... that's really odd. I can't see it."

"Oh Laura, wasn't he beautiful!"

"Magnificent. Only I can't understand where he's got to."

"He didn't half give me a fright," Bethan said, giggling nervously. "Sneaking up on us like that."

"Me too," Laura agreed. "Just imagine if he'd been on *this* side of the fence!"

Bethan gave a little shriek and ran down the slope again. "Come on. Let's go home. I'm starving."

"And me," Laura said, hitching her camera case on to her shoulder. But before leaving, she glanced back, hoping to spot the wolf again.

But there was no sign. It had vanished as quickly as it had appeared.

On Saturday morning, Laura and Bethan called for Gary again. He stood in his doorway and pulled a face. "Do I have to come? I want to go and see Kess."

"It's your project as much as ours," Bethan argued. "You've got to come."

"It'll take your mind off things," Laura said hopefully. "There's all sorts of animals there. It'll be great."

He heaved a sigh. "OK, but I don't want to be too long. Kess needs me."

They walked briskly towards the rare breeds park, the frosty air sharp on their faces. Overhead, watery sunlight filtered down, turning the entire countryside into shimmering, sparkling crystal.

Bethan burst into song. "*We're walking in a winter wonderland…*"

Gary glared unappreciatively.

"Being grumpy is going to help no one," Bethan remarked.

"We saw a wolf yesterday," Laura told him, hoping to cheer him up. "It scared us to death."

But he was miles away, walking along, hands stuffed in his pockets, head down. Laura and Bethan glanced at each other and sighed.

The gates of Cottesbrook Rare Breeds Park

stood open. The stone eagles didn't look half so unfriendly and Laura, Bethan and Gary walked down the drive to the ticket kiosk.

An old chap in a thick warm coat, scarf and fingerless gloves peered out from the kiosk. Cosy in there with his flask of coffee and sandwiches, he said, "Three children?"

"I don't think we have to pay," Laura explained hopefully. "We're doing a school project. Colonel Cartwright-Holmes knows all about it."

"Ah, that's you lot, is it?" he said, sipping his coffee from a plastic cup. "Go on, in you go. Colonel's expecting you."

"Thanks," Laura smiled, squeezing through the turnstile. "How do we find him?"

"If he's not around, go through a gate marked private. His house is on the other side of that." He took a bite of sandwich. "He won't be far."

"How will we know him?"

"Can't miss him. Big bloke, six foot odd, shoulders out here," he said stretching his arms as far as the kiosk would allow. "Sheep-skin jacket, green wellies. Probably smoking a big cigar. And like as not he'll have an African gent with him – Bhooto. He'll be wearing his camouflage outfit, I imagine."

Laura glanced at Bethan. "Sounds like the two unloading that lorry yesterday afternoon."

They hadn't gone more than a couple of steps when they were approached by two men who fitted that description perfectly.

The bigger man put aside his fat cigar and extended a large puffy hand. "I imagine you're the kids doing a project on endangered species. Am I right?"

"Yes, that's us," Laura smiled.

"Jeffrey Cartwright-Holmes," he introduced himself, shaking Laura's hand. "And this is Bhooto, my right-hand man."

Laura smiled at the hefty black-skinned man, who looked the three of them over briefly before dismissing them as unimportant.

Nevertheless she introduced her friends enthusiastically. "Pleased to meet you. I'm Laura. This is Bethan and Gary."

Bethan shook hands but to Laura's embarrassment, Gary just grunted and kept his hands in his pockets.

Laura nudged him. "Gary!" she hissed.

Reluctantly he shook hands, but it seemed an effort. She felt like shaking him, particularly when she saw the Colonel give him a curious look. She couldn't blame him. Yet it was odd. Gary wasn't usually rude to people.

Embarrassed at getting off to a bad start, she was relieved that the Colonel didn't seem unduly worried. He began the tour, talking non-stop about his animals, their background, and how he came to have them.

Bethan took notes and Laura took photographs, while Gary dawdled behind with a sullen expression on his face.

"What are these?" Laura asked as she saw the Colonel giving Gary another curious look.

"These?" he said, turning back to the girls. "These are Arctic foxes. Found mostly in the Arctic Circle, as you would imagine. Come back and see them in the summer and they'll be a smokey grey-brown colour instead of white. And these," he added, moving on, "are African wild dogs, rapidly facing extinction. There's probably only around 5,000 of them left anywhere in the world."

"And that's not a real hill at all," Laura remarked, pointing beyond the pack of large pointed-eared dogs to the grassy mound in the middle of the enclosure.

"What did you say?" The Colonel rounded on her, while Bhooto, who had seemed bored by the whole proceedings, suddenly jerked to attention.

They were both staring at her and she felt a prickle of discomfort. "We ... er ... saw you unloading some crates into it yesterday," she stammered, noticing that a nerve had started ticking at the corner of the Colonel's eye. "It's one of those bunkers from the war, isn't it?"

The two men continued to stare.

Bethan smiled nervously. "We thought it was very environmentally friendly," she joked.

No one laughed.

"We were just taking a few photos of the park as a whole," Laura went on, wishing she'd kept her mouth shut about the bunker. They were obviously not meant to know about it.

"You took photographs..."

Bhooto took a step towards them, a look on his face that made the girls back off.

The Colonel placed a hand lightly on his arm and their eyes met briefly. A secret message seemed to pass between them.

"Top secret, is it?" said Gary suddenly.

It was the first time he'd spoken since arriving here. Now everyone turned to stare. There was a strange look on his face. Almost like – hatred!

But the Colonel's face broke into a smile. His teeth were yellow. "Top secret? Hardly. Just foodstuffs. And yes, Laura, you're quite right, it is an old war bunker. Makes an excellent store room." He rubbed his hands together. "Now, any more questions?"

"I've got a question!" Gary announced.

Laura groaned inwardly. Now what?

Gary looked squarely at the Colonel. It *was* hatred in his face! Coldly he asked, "Do you actually like animals, Colonel?"

"Gary!" Laura hissed, horrified by his question.

But the Colonel simply smiled indulgently. "It's quite all right. The boy has asked a perfectly good question. For all you know, maybe I couldn't care less if certain species became extinct. Maybe I go abroad just for fun. Maybe I run this place just to get rich."

"And do you?" asked Gary.

Laura was beginning to feel sick. This was not how she intended this visit to go.

The Colonel seemed bemused. "Well firstly, no one could get rich running this place. It costs more to run than I make. Secondly, I don't like flying, so I wouldn't go abroad unless I really needed to. And thirdly..." his expression changed. He looked deadly serious. "The protection of animals and their preservation is the single most important thing in my life. It *is* my life!"

No one spoke. No one moved. The words seemed to hang in the air while everyone absorbed them.

Then he looked at Laura. "Do carry on taking your photographs, m'dear."

Not sure whether he meant for her to photograph the African wild dogs or him, she nervously fiddled with her camera.

"Oh no," she murmured.

"What?" hissed Bethan.

"I've run out of film."

"Didn't you bring another one?"

Laura shook her head. "I shouldn't have taken so many pictures last night."

The Colonel stepped forward. "Give me your camera. I'll nip back to the house and put a new film in for you."

"Oh! Thank you," she murmured, feeling awkward.

"Feel free to wander around," he said pleasantly, as if the last few embarrassing moments had never happened. He marched off, Bhooto hot on his heels.

Laura glared at Gary. "What has got into you? You were really rude to the Colonel!"

"Yes," Bethan agreed. "That was a pretty awful question to ask him. Of course he likes animals. He runs this place, doesn't he?"

"Yeah, he runs this place, but I bet it's not for the good of the animals," Gary said angrily. "He's up to something. See how they reacted about the bunker?"

"Yes, that was odd, but..."

Gary's eyes blazed. "He's not an animal lover. Believe me!"

Laura was beginning to lose patience. "Why isn't he?"

"Because," said Gary, "a true animal lover wouldn't knock a dog down and leave it lying injured in the road."

"What!" both girls cried together.

Gary's face was ashen. "That's right, he's the one. The Colonel's the one who knocked Kess down and didn't stop to help. Still think he cares about animals?"

Chapter 4

"The Colonel!" Laura gasped. "The Colonel knocked your dog down! Are you sure?"

"How come he hasn't recognized you?"

"It was freezing the day it happened. I'd got my hood down over my eyes and my scarf round my mouth," Gary explained. "Anyway, he wasn't interested in me or Kess. All he cared about was his car."

"Are you going to tell him?" Bethan asked.

Gary stared off into the distance. "Oh, he'll know it's me all right — when I get my revenge."

Warily Laura asked, "What exactly are you going to do?"

He shrugged. "Don't know yet. But I'm definitely going to let people know what he's really like. Protector of animals — that's a laugh!"

"Gary..." Laura said anxiously. "Maybe you should just tell him who you are. See what he has to say."

"I know what he'll say. He'll say all the right things, because you lot are around. He'll probably even offer to buy me another dog!"

"You don't know that..."

"I do!" Gary cried. "I know he's a smarmy creep who doesn't give a hoot about animals."

Bethan folded her arms. "So why does he bother with all this?"

"Because he's making money out of it — somehow," Gary argued.

"How exactly?" Bethan demanded. "He hasn't made much out of us, we got in free. And it's not exactly teeming with paying customers, is it?"

Gary glared stubbornly. "I said *somehow*."

"Stop arguing, will you!" Laura interrupted. "Come on, let's look at the animals. That is why we're here." She spotted someone going into a large cage which, according to the plaque, contained Tasmanian Devils – fierce, carnivorous marsupials from Tasmania. "Let's go and see what he's doing."

He was about nineteen, tall and broad with floppy blond hair and a kind face. He talked softly to the rodent-like creatures as he filled their food bowls. They responded by cheekily stealing the food from his hands.

"Hi! They seem to like you. Don't they bite?" Laura asked, as he came out, locking the cage behind him.

"They don't bite me," he shrugged, as if the thought had never occurred to him.

"We're doing a project on endangered species," Laura told him. "What do you do here?"

He thought for a second. "Me? I feed the animals, look after them. I mend things. I give all the animals names ... even the birds."

"And what's your name?" Bethan asked, ready to jot it down with her other notes.

He leant over her notepad. "I'm called Matty – Matthew Johnson. Shall I spell it for you?"

"No, it's OK," Bethan said cheerfully.

Laura smiled at him. "It must be great knowing you're helping to protect endangered animals."

"Someone's got to protect them," he answered simply. "He don't pay me much, but I can't go nowhere else. They need me."

"The animals?" Bethan mused and Matty nodded his head vigorously.

"What's the Colonel like to work for?" Gary asked innocently.

"Don't like him," Matty replied swiftly. Then he put his hand over Bethan's notepad. "Don't write that down. He'll sack me. And I don't want to lose my job here."

"Why don't you like the Colonel?" Gary asked.

Matty looked nervous. His dark brown eyes darted this way and that. "Sorry, I've got to go. Dot and Daisy need fresh hay."

Without another word he loped off across the park towards the stables.

Gary arched his eyebrows. "See! Colonel whatsisname is not all he's cracked up to be. There's something definitely dodgy about that bloke... Watch out, they're coming back."

The Colonel strolled over and handed Laura a roll of film and her camera while Bhooto stood behind him, looking grim.

"There you are, one roll of used film. And a new film in your camera."

"Thank you."

The guided tour continued. Bethan filled page after page of notes and Laura kept snapping away, but all the time on edge in case Gary came out with a question like, why doesn't Matty Johnson like you? Although, to be truthful, she wanted to know the answer to that question herself.

It started to snow again. The sky had darkened to an ominous shade of greyish-white, and everyone was beginning to turn blue.

"If you've seen enough, kids," said the Colonel, "I think we should stop now before the weather gets any worse. You can always come back another day if you need more information."

But there was one animal that Laura just had to see again before they left.

Eagerly she asked, "Could we just see the white wolf before we go, please?"

Bhooto, who had been walking ahead of them, stopped dead. They all practically barged into him. He spun round, a look of terror in his eyes.

"What white wolf?" the Colonel asked. "We don't have a white wolf. Not any more." He sounded annoyed and glanced in Matty's direction. "We *should* have had a white wolf, but unfortunately, the only pure white wolf we ever had died as a cub about a year ago."

Laura was totally confused. "But we saw a wolf."

"Not here you didn't," the Colonel stated, clapping a hand on Bhooto's shoulder. "And I should be careful what you say. You'll be giving Bhooto here nightmares. What you saw was probably an Arctic fox."

"But it wasn—" Laura began, but Gary interrupted her.

"Nightmares? Why, is Bhooto scared of wolves or something?"

"Bhooto was brought up in the heart of

Africa," said the Colonel. "He's a bit superstitious when it comes to animals dying. Tends to believe the animal's spirit can come back and haunt you."

"Why would it do that?" Gary asked inquisitively. "He didn't have anything to do with its death, did he?"

"Gary!" Laura hissed.

The Colonel's face creased into a smile, and his hand came heavily down on Gary's shoulder. "The boy doesn't pull any punches, does he? Straight to the point. I like that."

Laura held her breath, afraid of what Gary would say or do next.

There was amusement in the Colonel's voice. "And no, Bhooto had nothing to do with the cub's death." His eyes flitted in Matty's direction again, and his tone changed. "But sadly we've no wolves here, neither real nor ghost."

Laura frowned. Just what was going on here? It was a wolf she and Bethan saw. And no ghost wolf either. That wolf had real fur and teeth!

The Colonel rubbed his hands together.

"Now then, what say we wind this up. I've business to attend to and you three look frozen."

With that, the two men turned and headed back towards the exit, distancing themselves from the children. Bhooto looked jittery and whispered frantically to the Colonel as they strode back up the park.

The Colonel seemed merely bemused and patted Bhooto's shoulder as if he was calming a fretful child.

"A wolf!" Gary scoffed as they followed some distance behind. "Don't you two know the difference between a wolf and a fox?"

"Yes, actually we do," Bethan argued. "And believe me, we definitely saw a wolf. A big, beautiful, ferocious, white wolf. Didn't we, Laura?"

"She's telling the truth. It was a wolf," Laura murmured vaguely. But something was puzzling her. All the animals here were safely locked up in cages and large enclosures. Yet that wolf had been roaming freely along by the fence.

Gary was still mocking them. "Wolf, fox …

sure it wasn't a rabbit you saw?"

"It was a wolf," Laura said quietly. "And I'll tell you something else. That wolf wasn't in a cage.

"It was running free!"

Chapter 5

"You don't get wolves running wild in England!" Gary mocked. "Hundreds of years ago maybe, but not any more."

"We saw one!" Bethan argued. "A big one!"

"You couldn't have."

Laura frowned. "Well, the idea of a wolf around here certainly freaked old Bhooto. He looked really spooked."

Bethan's blue eyes twinkled mischievously. "Perhaps it was a ghost wolf!"

Laura and Gary laughed.

"Could be," she went on. "Maybe it was the spirit of the wolf that died. Maybe its ghost does haunt this place... Ah, that's what I need," she said, changing the subject as they walked past the public toilets. "Wait for me. I've got to go."

She didn't get far. "Oh no! Out of order. Burst pipes."

"You'll just have to wait," Laura told her. But Bethan had other ideas.

"Do you think Colonel Cartwright-Holmes would let me use his loo?"

Laura shrugged. "Go and ask him before he goes in."

Bethan raced after the Colonel, catching him up just as he was about to go through a gate marked private. She anxiously pointed out that the public toilets were out of order.

He sighed, seeming less than enthusiastic. Nevertheless, he led the way through the gate and into his own private part of the park.

His garden was beautiful, and his house was a huge old mansion that could almost have belonged to another age.

Gary softly whistled.

It was secluded and quiet. High walls shielded the garden from the outside world and Laura had the distinct impression that they were very privileged to be here.

The Colonel led the way up a crooked path to a back door. "Leave your shoes outside, would you?"

In stocking feet they followed the Colonel and Bhooto into the house. It felt warm and luxurious, and deep-pile carpets smothered their toes.

Bhooto immediately disappeared into one of the rooms, still muttering to himself.

"Poor man," the Colonel remarked, showing Bethan up the stairs to the bathroom and Laura and Gary into the sitting room. "He's so superstitious. Excuse me a moment while I speak to him."

Left alone, they gazed in wonder around the room.

Gary gave another long, low whistle. "Has this guy got money or what!"

"Oh wow!" Laura murmured, looking all around.

The suite was of white leather, and the room was filled with treasures from all over the world. Huge Chinese vases, oriental rugs, African carvings, fabulous oil paintings of elephants and wildlife. Life-sized statues of leopards and jaguars, and a whole mass of other ornaments and trinkets.

"This is unbelievable!"

Gary wandered around the room, picking up some of the smaller ornaments. "How on earth does a rare breeds park pay for all this — *and* his trips abroad?"

Laura shrugged. "I've no idea."

Bethan peeped around the door then. "Ah, there you are. Thought I heard voices." Her mouth dropped open at the sight of the rich furnishings. "What a house — and you should see his bathroom."

"What's it like?" Laura asked inquisitively.

"Gold plated taps, marble everywhere and..."

"I was right!" Gary interrupted them and the girls spun round to stare at him.

"Right about what?" Bethan asked.

He looked deadly serious. "He doesn't care about animals and endangered species at all."

Bethan groaned. "Why? Just because he's got a posh house?"

"No, not that. Here..." he handed a little ornament to Laura and a pen holder to Bethan.

"What?" Laura puzzled, studying the small, heavy figurine.

Gary's eyes blazed. "Can't you see? The pen holder is made of horn, and that ornament is made out of ivory. Horn comes from antelopes and ivory comes from elephants! They kill the animals to get those things.

"Call that the actions of someone who's trying to protect endangered animals? Because I don't!"

Chapter 6

"Ah! I see you're admiring my trinkets," Colonel Cartwright-Holmes said suddenly, stepping into the room behind them.

Laura, Bethan and Gary swung round, startled.

"And I imagine you're wondering what someone like me – protector of wildlife – is doing with ornaments made from ivory and the like."

"Yeah! That did cross our minds!" Gary said defiantly, folding his arms and staring hard at the Colonel.

The Colonel sauntered into the centre of the room and picked up an ivory figurine. "Then I shall tell you." He took a deep breath. "I keep this sort of thing around to remind me of how vital our work here is. Ivory poaching has to stop. We don't need this kind of junk. What we need is a safe environment for the elephant to live and thrive. And not just the elephant, but all the animals in danger of being wiped off the face of the earth through man's greed."

He went silent, but stood there, his face ravaged with anger and misery as he stared in disgust at the ivory ornament. Laura wondered if she ought to take his picture.

And then he replaced the ornament on his coffee table and sighed. "These were actually gifts from someone who didn't know better. An old aunt who thought because I was interested in wildlife, I'd like some ornaments made from their horns and tusks." He shook his head sadly. "She meant well, bless her. And the only reason I didn't throw them away in disgust is in case I ever forget how important our work is."

Bethan cast him a huge smile. "That explains it then."

"Yes," Laura agreed, having the strangest

feeling that his little speech was a bit too well rehearsed. "It's time we were going. Thank you for all your help, Colonel."

"My pleasure," he said, shaking the girls by the hand. Gary turned aside to admire a painting just as the Colonel headed for him. Laura's eyes fluttered shut in embarrassment.

"So," said the Colonel, changing direction and holding the door for them, "if you'd collect your shoes from the back... There's no access to the road from the rear of my house, so you'll have to go out the front."

They picked up their shoes from the back doorstep, then followed him back through the house to the front door. He unlocked it with a key from his keyring.

Moments later they were out in the cold and heading home.

Gary spoke first. "I suppose you two believed him."

"It sounded reasonable enough," Laura admitted.

Bethan frowned at Gary. "Well, I believed him, and you were really rude to him, Gary."

"What do you expect!" Gary blazed. "He

almost killed Kess... Oh, anyway, I'm going to the vet's to see how she is."

"We'll come too," Laura said, catching him up as he strode off towards Coopers Lane.

They talked and argued non-stop until they reached the vet's surgery on the High Street. Two people were sitting in the waiting room: a woman with a big ginger cat and a little boy who sat whispering into the cardboard box he was clutching.

Gary went straight up to the reception desk. "Hello Rachel. How's Kess?"

The nurse gave him a reassuring smile. "She's doing fine. I see you've brought some friends to see her. She'll like that."

"I couldn't get here earlier. We had to go to the rare breeds park to do a project."

"Did you?" Rachel remarked, leading the way through to a back room. "My brother works there. Matty – tall, blond hair. Did you see him?"

"Yes, we met him," Laura said, thinking what a small world it was.

The nurse smiled. She looked quite similar to her brother. The same blonde hair and soft voice. "Matty absolutely adores animals. If he'd been the brainy type he might have become a vet himself. But he's not too good at exams and things."

They entered the recovery room. It was bright and airy with a number of wooden compartments with wire fronts. All empty except for one.

A beautiful golden-brown and white collie lay with her eyes half closed, looking very sorry for herself.

Laura's heart lurched.

Normally, Kess would greet everyone by jumping up and barking and licking them to death. Now she couldn't even wag her tail.

Gary knelt down and opened up the front of the cage.

"Kess ... hello girl. How are you?"

Laura and Bethan looked sadly at each other.

The nurse was the only cheerful face in the room. "Look at you all. I thought you'd come to cheer Kess up."

They all made a fuss of Kess then, but she could hardly keep her eyes open.

Gary sat close, stroking her beautiful head and talking softly to her. Tears sprang up in Bethan's eyes and she dashed out of the room.

"So," Rachel said to Laura, "You've been to Cottesbrook Park. What did you think about it?"

"It was interesting..." Laura began. But Gary interrupted.

"Yeah – very interesting!" he said angrily. "One of the things we discovered was that the owner was the person who knocked Kess down."

"Cartwright-Holmes?" said Rachel in a cold voice. "That doesn't surprise me."

Laura stared at her. "Why doesn't it?"

She bit her lip and looked away awkwardly. "Oh well, nothing really. Just things I've heard."

"What things?" demanded Gary.

The nurse hesitated, chewing her lip nervously. "I shouldn't say really. My brother works there, remember. I'd hate him to lose his job. Those animals are his life."

Laura was wildly curious. "We won't say anything, we promise."

Rachel twisted her fingers together nervously. "Well, I know the Colonel has a reputation for doing great things for the preservation of wildlife. He's so well known, yet…"

"Yet what?" Laura begged.

"Yet…" she lowered her voice. "From what Matty has told me, the Colonel has a cruel streak. A very cruel streak."

"What's Matty said?" Laura asked inquisitively.

Rachel looked flustered. "Nothing. Forget it. I've said too much already." She made an effort then to change the subject. "So, you saw all the animals this afternoon. That must have been nice."

"Yes … well, almost all of them," Laura answered, thinking about the wolf. "The day before, my friend and I saw a wolf. But the Colonel says there are no wolves."

Rachel turned pale. "A wolf?"

"Yes, a beautiful white wolf."

"Where did you see it?"

"Just inside the fence," Laura answered. "It sort of just appeared. When I tried to photograph it, it ran away."

"Where did it go?"

"I don't know," Laura shrugged. "I asked the Colonel about it, and he said the only wolf they had died as a cub."

A look of horror flashed briefly across Rachel's face. "You told the Colonel?"

"Yes. Why not?" Laura puzzled.

"Oh, no reason," Rachel said awkwardly. "Er … I remember the wolf cub dying. It was about a year ago. Matty told me all about it."

"So what did we see?" Laura asked, completely baffled. "A wild wolf?"

"Maybe an Arctic fox got loose," Rachel suggested.

"That's what I said," Gary piped up.

"It wasn't a fox!" Laura argued. "It was definitely a wolf — and he was so magnificent."

The nurse shrugged, almost disinterested. "Well, I shouldn't worry about it. And I certainly wouldn't mention it to the Colonel again. Now I have to get back to reception. Stay as long as you like."

Laura stood, feeling totally confused. A huge white wolf was wandering freely around the park, and no one seemed to take it seriously.

It was as if everyone wanted to pretend it didn't exist. But it did exist. That wolf was real.

And it was dangerous!

Chapter 7

Leaving Gary with Kess, Laura and Bethan headed towards the photo shop. Laura couldn't wait to get her first roll of film developed. After dropping it in, they went along to the library in town to get some books on endangered species for their project.

"We could go back to my house if you like," Bethan suggested, wrinkling her nose. "Only as it's Saturday my sisters will be fighting over the hair drier and the bathroom and who's pinched whose make-up."

"Come to mine then," said Laura.

Bethan beamed. "Can I hold your baby brother?"

"Five minutes only!" Laura warned. "We've

got to do some work on this project. I don't think Gary's going to add much to it."

An icy wind whistled in off the moors as they turned into Laura's street. She pulled up her collar. "Look at that sky, Beth. We're in for some heavy snow."

"Lovely! I love the snow." She burst into song. "*I'm dreaming of a white Christmas...*"

"Christmas was ages ago," Laura remarked, loving the snow herself. The only problem would be for the birds and little animals trying to find food under a thick blanket of snow.

And not just the *little* animals.

"Beth, what do wolves eat?"

"Wolves?" Bethan answered, spreading her fingers like claws. "Wolves eat people, of course!"

Once indoors, Bethan went all gooey-eyed over baby Jonathan while Laura sat at the table and began leafing through the library books.

"How did it go, girls?" Laura's mother asked in between carrying the freshly ironed laundry upstairs.

"OK I suppose," said Laura. "Except the owner was the man who knocked Kess down, so Gary wasn't at all happy."

"I shouldn't think he was. How is Kess?"

The girls exchanged glances. "She doesn't look too well actually," Laura said sadly.

"That's a shame," her mother replied. "She's a lovely dog."

Laura made a start on their project: listing as many species of endangered animals as she could find and drawing maps of the places they lived. Bethan eventually felt guilty at leaving her to do all the work and joined her.

"Look! A chapter on wolves," she announced after a while.

"Let's see…"

A full-page colour photograph of a wolf stared out at them.

Laura caught her breath.

The wolf was grey. Not snowy-white like their wolf. But it had those same clear amber eyes. The lolling tongue. The strong white fangs.

"It says here," Bethan began, reading the text, "a wolf can bolt up to one-fifth of its own weight at a sitting. Hence the expression, 'to wolf one's food'. Its food ranges from elk, reindeer and cattle, to cats, mice and fruit." She grinned at Laura. "Says nothing about eating people. I suppose they're a delicacy."

Laura tried to drag her eyes away from the wolf's. But they seemed to mesmerize her. It was incredible that one of these animals was roaming loose in a wildlife park – and no one seemed to be taking it seriously. Except her.

She tried not to think about what Bethan had said – she was only joking about wolves eating people.

But what if it wasn't a joke…

What if wolves really did eat people!

Chapter 8

By Monday afternoon the snow was falling in big fat snowflakes. A soft white carpet smothered streets and rooftops and trees, as beautiful as a scene from a Christmas card.

The moors however resembled the Antarctic, and Laura was glad to get in out of the cold.

"I'm home, Mum — and it's freezing out!" she called, throwing off her hat, gloves and coat as the warmth of the house curled around her.

Little Jonathan was gurgling happily in his baby bouncer. Laura knelt down and gave him a kiss.

"Hello sweetie…" she said, disentangling his chubby hands from her hair.

Her mother came in from the kitchen. "Bad news about your film, I'm afraid."

"Oh?"

"Nothing's come out. Completely blank."

"Nothing?" Laura wailed.

"The girl in the shop said the film had been exposed to the light. Didn't you follow Uncle Eddie's instructions when you took the film out?"

"I didn't take it out. Colonel Cartwright-Holmes did it."

Her mother frowned. "Well, he's ruined it for you. What an awful shame."

Laura slumped into a chair. All those pictures of the open bunker. The men unloading those crates. The lovely views of the park. All wasted! How on earth did the Colonel manage to ruin her film? Surely a man like him knew how to change a film?

It was much later that night, when the thought occurred to her. Just as she was drifting off to sleep, she recalled the way the Colonel and Bhooto had looked at her after learning she'd photographed them putting the crates in the bunker.

They hadn't been pleased. That bunker, or whatever they stored in there, was secret. *Their* secret.

It wasn't for people like her to know about. And it certainly wasn't for people to photograph!

Wide awake now, she stared at the ceiling. It was almost unbelievable…

But had the Colonel ruined her film deliberately?

Gary listened carefully to her at school the next day. His eyes were cold.

"So, what do you think?" Laura repeated. "Do you reckon the Colonel wrecked my film on purpose? Is their secret bunker so secret that they destroyed the pictures I took of it?"

"It wouldn't surprise me," Gary answered.

Bethan leant closer, whispering so their teacher couldn't hear. "He wouldn't do that. I mean, why should he?"

"Because he's up to something," Gary hissed. "Him and Bhooto were really annoyed when Laura told them she'd taken photographs. So what does the Colonel do? Buzzes off with her camera to change the film. Very convenient!"

Bethan wrinkled her nose. "I still don't think he'd ruin it on purpose."

Their teacher peered over her spectacles at them. "I hope all this talking is about your project. Not just idle chit-chat."

"No, Miss," Laura answered. Then lowered her voice. "Anyway I'm going to re-take them. Today after school. Anyone coming with me?"

The snow lay in drifts – deep against the park wall, more shallow where the forest trees provided shelter. It crunched softly underfoot as Laura, Bethan and Gary trudged through it later that afternoon.

Silvery icicles dangled from branches, sparkling in the watery sunlight. And frost illuminated the spiders' webs, transforming them into giant diamonds dotted amongst the shrubbery.

A crystal forest, Laura thought, delighting in the glorious beauty of it all.

"When the snowman brings the snow…"

Bethan sang cheerfully as they waded through the snow.

"Here he comes!" Gary shouted, jumping up to shake the snow from a branch over her head.

She responded with an accurately aimed snowball. Gary threw one back and a massive snowball fight erupted between the three of them.

By the time they reached the fence at the end of the wall they looked like snowmen themselves. But it was good to see Gary having fun again.

Laura scrambled up the slope which looked out over the park. "This is where we saw the wolf," she told Gary.

"Fox!" he corrected her.

"Wolf!" both she and Bethan echoed.

"Yeah, yeah," he mocked. "You'll be seeing Little Red Riding Hood next."

Laura pulled a face at him as she got her camera ready. "I just hope the Colonel's put this film in right."

She took a few photographs and then groaned. "These won't be half as good as the first lot. That bunker looks like a hill. There's nothing going on down there. No lorry. No crates getting unloaded. It's boring!"

Bethan struggled up after her. "Never mind. You probably got some nice pictures of animals the other day."

"If they come out," Laura remarked warily.

"It makes you wonder, doesn't it?" Gary said, leaning against the fence, hands shoved into his pockets.

"What does?"

"What he was so secretive about. I mean, destroying your film is a bit like destroying evidence."

"Evidence!" Bethan exclaimed. "Gary, what are you talking about?"

"It's obvious. He doesn't want any photographs of that stuff being delivered here — whatever it was."

"He said it was animal food," Bethan reminded him. "Hardly a crime."

Laura recalled how they'd struggled to get the crate off the lorry. "It weighed a ton, Beth. Remember, they had to use a fork-lift truck."

"A ton of straw weighs the same as a ton of gold," Bethan said haughtily.

"Shut up, clever clogs!" Gary grinned, throwing another snowball at her.

But suddenly Beth's laughter died, her smile froze.

Gary followed her gaze as Laura busied herself with her camera.

In a hushed voice Gary said, "Er ... Laura ... I hope you've got some film left."

"A bit, why?"

He gulped and she glanced at him – and then at Bethan. They looked like two frozen ice statues. They were staring straight past her. Towards the forest. "What's up? You two look like you've seen a ghost."

"No ... not a ghost," Gary croaked. "But I have to admit, it's not a fox either."

"What?" Laura breathed, as an icy shiver ran down her spine. She turned slowly, fear clawing its way up to her throat.

And then she saw it.

The wolf was standing a short distance off amongst the trees. A huge, fearfully beautiful beast. Its thick coat as white as the snow. Its nose and lips shiny black. Tongue lolling over sharp white fangs. Clear, bright eyes – fixed on them.

Laura gasped.

There was no safety barrier dividing them this time. Predator and prey were on the same side of the fence. The wolf wasn't just roaming free around the park – it was *completely* free!

Her thoughts raced.

Would it attack? Would it risk attacking three of them? What did Bethan say they ate?

People!

"No!" she breathed. It couldn't ... could it?

A wolf can eat one fifth of its own weight in one sitting ... wolfing its food ... eat like a wolf...

Oh grandmamma – what big teeth you have...

Chapter 9

The wolf didn't flinch. It stood openly watching them. Taking a long, long look. Then it raised its head, sniffing the air, catching their scent.

"Take its picture," Gary hissed.

"Oh sure!" Laura uttered, wanting to run, only too petrified to turn her back on it. "Will you ask it to say cheese, or will I?"

"Just take its picture," he ordered again.

"I can't. My hands are shaking too much."

"Try!"

Slowly, very slowly, Laura raised the camera to her eye. But instantly, the wolf backed off, drawing back its lips in a snarl.

"Oh God!" Laura breathed, her knees

buckling.

But instead of lunging at them, the wolf turned tail and loped off through the trees.

Gary grabbed her camera and began snapping away like mad. "Got it, I think."

Bethan clutched Laura's arm. She was trembling from head to foot. "I thought we'd had it! I thought it was going to attack us."

Laura clung to her. "I knew it shouldn't have been just wandering freely around the park. I knew it!"

"We've got to tell someone," Bethan murmured, her eyes wide with fright.

"And who'll believe us?"

Gary patted the camera. "They'll have to believe this, won't they?"

Laura looked doubtful. "That's if the film comes out. Don't forget who put it in!"

They hurried back towards the start of the forest. Or tried to hurry. The deep snow made walking slow and difficult. And all the while there was the fear that the wolf could come sneaking back at any minute.

Eventually they reached the road and began the slow trek to the photo shop. Roads were icy and slushy now and they reached the shop breathless and cold.

Laura asked the assistant if she would take the film out for her. She wanted no mistakes this time.

"No problem," the girl smiled, showing her how it was done.

"My last film got ruined. The light got in," Laura explained.

"Ah, that was you, was it?"

Laura nodded and Gary leant on the counter. "How do you reckon the light got in?" he asked.

"Opening the camera without winding the film back first, I guess," the assistant suggested. Then she looked thoughtful. "Only that would just make your pictures fog. As I recall, your entire film was ruined."

"So how could that have happened?" Laura asked, puzzled.

The girl nibbled a thumbnail for a moment. "The only thing I can think of is that someone pulled the whole film out, then rewound it. You didn't, did you?"

"No, I didn't," Laura replied, glancing at

her friends. Their expressions mirrored her own thoughts.

She didn't do it. But they knew a man who might have!

"He's definitely up to something!" Gary declared as they trudged towards the vet's. "The Colonel is hiding something – and I bet it's illegal. That's how he's so rich. I bet his rare breeds park is just a cover-up, so he can travel the world. I bet he's an international drug smuggler!"

"Oh Gary, stop exaggerating," Bethan groaned. "He's either just a clever business-man, or he was born rich."

"But he destroyed our evidence!" Gary argued.

"Evidence!" Bethan wailed. "Evidence that his llamas eat straw? And his African wild dogs eat meat? Big deal! Those crates were full of animal food, and he uses that bunker as a cold storage room."

"He stores his illegal drugs in there," Gary stated.

Laura ignored them, lost in her own

thoughts. It certainly seemed that the Colonel destroyed her film on purpose. But she honestly didn't think he was a drug smuggler. He probably just kept expensive goods or equipment in that bunker. And if people knew he stored things there, he might get burgled. He probably just preferred to keep his business private.

Besides, at the moment, she had other things to worry about. Like a beautiful but very dangerous wolf living wild. Living just a mile from her home.

Today there had been three of them, together. The wolf hadn't attacked. But what if it had been just one person, alone?

And the wolf was hungry…

Chapter 10

By morning snow lay knee deep. Icicles hung from window ledges and traffic slid to a standstill. The school's plumbing and heating system froze solid and everyone was sent home.

After dropping off their school bags at Laura's house, she and Bethan decided to see if the photographs had come out this time.

Laura's mother waved from the door. "Watch out for the wolves!" she laughed.

The two girls exchanged glances.

"Even *she* thinks we're imagining things," Laura said miserably. "She reckons it was just a dog — a German Shepherd or a husky or something."

Bethan wrinkled her nose. "Suppose it could have been. Let's just hope the photos have come out. At least she'll see that we saw *something*."

"We saw a wolf!" Laura reminded her. "Not a fox or a dog – a wolf!"

"OK," Bethan agreed. "OK."

The photo shop assistant smiled. "Success! Looks like they've all come out this time."

Relieved, Laura paid for them, and quickly skimmed through the pictures she'd taken in the park. She'd got some nice shots of the animals. But the bunker looked nothing more than a little hill.

In the next photographs, the trees were slanted at an angle because of the way Gary had snatched the camera off her. She felt a twinge of disappointment.

He'd managed to photograph the wolf. But only as it was running away. Its white fur merged perfectly in with the snowy scenery.

"It doesn't look like anything," Laura groaned disappointedly. "You can tell it's not a fox. But it could be a dog."

"An expert might be able to tell the difference," Bethan suggested. "We could show the Colonel ... see what he says."

"I don't think so, Beth. He's already told us the only wolf they had died as a cub. And Bhooto was really odd about the thought of a wolf hanging about."

"But he would know for certain," Bethan argued. "He's an expert on wildlife."

Laura looked steadily at her friend. "We don't need an expert to tell us what we saw. We *know* we saw a wolf."

"But we need someone to believe us, so something can be done about it."

"Oh, I don't know, Beth," Laura sighed. "Have you forgotten what Rachel at the vet's said? That we shouldn't bother the Colonel about the wolf."

"Who else can we tell then?" Bethan shrugged. "If we tell the police, they might just hunt it down and kill it. At least the Colonel will give it a home in his park – wouldn't he?"

Laura thought for a moment. "Yes, I imagine so. Actually, he might be quite glad to own a wolf again. Remember how annoyed he looked when he talked about the wolf cub dying."

Bethan beamed. "So we'll go and show him the photos then, and see what he says?"

Casting aside any doubts she had, she nodded. "Yes, why not? It can't do any harm."

"Shall we see if Gary wants to come with us?"

Laura wrinkled her nose. "I'd rather keep him and the Colonel apart! Still, we'd better tell him our plans. I want to see how Kess is anyway."

They found Gary giving Kess's bedding a good shake in his back garden.

"Hi! You look busy," greeted Laura.

"I'm making everything nice for when Kess comes home," Gary answered.

Bethan beamed. "She's getting better!"

"Well, the vet says there's no change," Gary dismissed. "But that means she's not any worse. So she'll be up and about any day now."

The girls glanced sadly at each other. Then,

brightly, Laura said, "We've just got those photos out. Look."

Gary gave the blanket one last shake, then laid it carefully in Kess's wicker basket in the kitchen. "Let's see then."

He looked unimpressed. "You should have snapped him when he was looking at us."

"I know," Laura wailed. "But I was too shocked at the time."

"We've decided to show the Colonel," Bethan said warily.

"What!" Gary exploded. "What do you want to speak to that creep again for?"

"We need someone to believe us about the wolf," Laura hastily explained. "If we tell the police they might just hunt it down and kill it. We reckon the Colonel will look after it properly."

Gary looked doubtful. "He had a wolf remember — a cub — and that died. Plus Bhooto is scared stiff of wolves and Rachel said we shouldn't bother him with stories about wolves. Maybe she knows something we don't." He shook his head. "I reckon we should just leave it."

"But what if it attacks someone?" Laura said anxiously.

"Or it might wander on to the road and get run over," added Bethan.

Gary turned away and fluffed up Kess's blanket again. For some minutes he was silent. Then reluctantly he muttered, "I suppose we can't just leave it to roam. It's bound to go on the road..." He heaved a sigh. "When are you going to see him?"

"Now, I suppose," said Laura.

He grabbed his coat. "Well, don't expect me to be nice to him, will you."

Deep snowdrifts reached halfway up the walls of Cottesbrook Rare Breeds Park. Everywhere was locked, bolted and silent.

Laura groaned. "So much for that idea!"

Gary nodded towards the forest. "We could go that way and see if we can spot someone through the fence."

Laura's eyes widened in horror. "Haven't you forgotten something, Gary? Something large and furry with big teeth!"

"It didn't attack us last time. Anyway, it's

probably miles away by now," Gary said, heading towards the trees. "Well, you coming or not? It was you two who wanted to see the Colonel in the first place, remember."

The girls looked at each other.

"Whose idea was it to bring him?" Bethan groaned.

"We can't let him go on his own," said Laura with a reluctant look on her face.

"Oh, come on then," Bethan moaned as she linked her arm through Laura's and caught him up. "But I think we need our heads examining!"

Nervously, they trudged along by the park wall, avoiding the deepest snowdrifts. All the while listening and watching for the wolf.

But the forest was still. The only sounds were the soft crunch of their boots in the snow, and the whispering of the trees.

"It's beautiful, isn't it," Laura murmured. "I love winters like this."

"Remember last year," said Gary. "We went sledging on Badger Hill. And Kess, sledging down on my lap."

Laura smiled. "Then she tugged the rope,

helping us drag the sledge back up the hill."

"It was brilliant, wasn't it," Gary said, his eyes growing misty.

Bethan wrapped her arm around his neck. "She'll be better and having fun with us again in no time, you'll see."

"You reckon?" Gary sighed.

"Course she will. So don't start looking on the black side," Laura told him firmly as they reached the end of the wall. "Oh look! There's the Colonel and Bhooto and Matty. They're mending the fence by the looks of it."

Bhooto spotted them first. He whispered in the Colonel's ear.

The Colonel glanced towards them sharply. He looked annoyed. Then he pasted a smile on his face and greeted them warmly. "Well, well! Back again. You three certainly take your school work seriously."

"Sorry to trouble you," Laura began uneasily. "Only we'd like you to look at some photographs."

Bhooto's eyes flashed warning messages to the Colonel.

"Photos?" puzzled the Colonel, his eye beginning to twitch.

"Yes. Some that we took the other day," Laura answered, wondering why Gary was nudging her in the back.

"They came out then?" asked the Colonel, his voice rising a little.

Gary jabbed her again.

She glanced from the Colonel to Bhooto. Both men looked stunned, Bhooto specially. He looked like he wanted to tear the photos out of her hand.

Suddenly Laura realized why Gary was nudging her.

They thought she was talking about that *first* roll of film! The one that had got ruined. They hadn't expected it to come out — because the Colonel had let the light get at it.

She caught Gary's eye. He was thinking the same as her.

The Colonel *had* wrecked that film. Deliberately!

But why?

Intrigued suddenly, Laura decided not to let the Colonel know that his secret — whatever his secret was – was safe. The film *was* ruined.

She wanted to see what he would do.

"Yes the photos came out great, thanks," she fibbed. "The first film was a bit foggy, but not too bad." She glanced at Bethan, praying she wouldn't say anything.

There was a puzzled look on her face but she kept quiet.

Laura smiled innocently. "But it's these photographs we wanted to show you. What sort of animal would you say this is?"

The question didn't sink in. There was a strange look on the Colonel's face, while Bhooto looked ready to explode.

"Sorry? What did you say?" stammered the Colonel.

"This animal," Laura said, pointing to the wolf. "It's not very clear. But what would you say it is?"

"I would say it's a dog," the Colonel said vaguely, his mind clearly elsewhere. "German Shepherd by the size of it."

"Not a wolf then?" Laura quizzed.

Bhooto suddenly staggered, as if he'd been hit.

"No, not a wolf," the Colonel dismissed, giving Bhooto a disapproving glance. "The last wolf living wild around here was in the seventeen hundreds."

"Wolves?" murmured Matty, wandering over to them. "Can I see?"

"Of course," said Laura, but the Colonel interrupted, a harsh twang to his voice.

"Think you know about wolves, do you, lad?"

Matty stopped dead, his eyes narrowed against the Colonel.

"I suggest you get on with what you do know," continued the Colonel. "Like checking this fence for holes."

Laura bit her lip, recalling what the veterinary nurse had said about the Colonel.

He has a cruel streak…

Laura studied him. He was big and powerful. The way he'd just spoken to Matty was unpleasant and unnecessary. The way he'd left Kess injured without trying to help was heartless.

Yes, he did have a cruel streak.

But she sensed there was something else

about him. Something bad. He *was* up to something. He'd destroyed her film of crates being stored in his secret bunker.

Like Gary said — he'd destroyed the evidence.

And maybe Gary was right too about this rare breeds park being just a cover-up for something else.

Something illegal.

Chapter 11

For the first time since meeting the Colonel and Bhooto, Laura felt a twinge of fear. If they were up to something illegal they would hardly let three kids ruin things for them.

They had wanted that first reel of film destroyed. It was stupid of her to make them think it wasn't.

Stupid and dangerous!

She looked at the Colonel. Although he smiled a lot, he had a hard face. And as for Bhooto – he looked wild. Crazy even.

She took a step backwards, glad there was a fence between them. "We have to go now. Thank you for all your help…"

"Wait!" the Colonel snapped. Then the smile returned. "You know, I'd love to see the other photos. Have you got them with you?"

Laura gulped. Gary nudged her again. "Er ... no. They're at home."

"Drop them in sometime, I'd be interested in seeing them," he said pleasantly. Too pleasantly.

She hesitated. "Well actually, they aren't *that* brilliant."

"I'd still like to see them," he persisted, his false smile twitching slightly.

It had gone too far. Taking a deep breath Laura said, "Actually, the first film didn't come out. The light had got in. I didn't like to tell you."

He believed her!

She saw the muscles in his face relax. Saw the look of relief pass between him and Bhooto.

The danger had passed.

Until Gary spoke up…

"Funny that, don't you think," he said suddenly. "Considering *you* took the film out for her."

Laura's eyes fluttered shut in despair. Don't, Gary! she cried out beneath her breath. These men could be dangerous!

But his anger about Kess was finally bubbling over.

He marched straight up to the Colonel, and stood with his nose against the fence, ignoring Laura's tugging on his coat.

"Considering you're the big wildlife expert," he continued, "I'm surprised you can't take a film out of a camera without ruining it. Didn't do it on purpose by any chance, did you?"

The Colonel's face reddened. Then his eyes narrowed as he glared down at Gary. "I know you, don't I? Yes – I thought there was something familiar about you the first time we met."

"Don't strain yourself," said Gary angrily. "I wouldn't expect someone as important as you to remember a little thing like knocking my dog down!"

"Of course!" exclaimed the Colonel. "You're the boy who didn't have his dog on a lead."

"Kess doesn't need a lead!" Gary shouted furiously. "She's a great dog. It was your mad driving that did it."

"Gary, don't," Laura breathed, holding on to his arm. "We have to go."

But there was no stopping Gary now. "You still don't care how she is, do you?"

"If you'd had her on a lead…"

"She nearly died!" Gary shouted. "She's got a broken leg and internal injuries… She still might not make it."

"Gary!" the girls cried, trying to drag him away. But his fingers were through the netting, like a wild animal, trying to get at the Colonel.

"If I were you," the Colonel remarked, speaking calmly to Laura, "I'd take your friend home before I lose my temper."

"Gary, come on," Laura begged.

But he only raised his voice more. "Call yourself an animal lover? You don't care anything about animals. And we reckon this whole place is just a cover-up. You're up to something, and we're going to find out what it is and tell the world!"

"Gary!" Laura hissed, dragging him away.

A deadly look spread across the Colonel's face.

Deadly and evil.

An icy shiver ran down Laura's spine. These men were dangerous. More dangerous than any wild animal.

Gary saw the transformation in him too, and he stepped back, out of reach. Although he still hadn't got everything off his chest.

"You don't care about animals. And you don't know anything about them either. You can't even tell the difference between a dog and a wolf!"

Bhooto looked agitated again, but the Colonel stepped calmly up to the fence. He spoke softly. But the threat came across loud and clear.

"Young man, I should think very carefully before you go making wild accusations about my work here. I won't have my reputation ruined." His eyes glinted dangerously. "That would really upset me."

"Gary, come on!" Laura begged, dragging him away. "I am sorry, Colonel, only he's very upset about Kess."

"I'm not scared of you," Gary shouted as the girls dragged him away. "I'm going to tell people what you're really like…"

"Gary, shut up!" Laura hissed.

"I should take your friend's advice, son," the Colonel said, looking deadly. "And keep your mouth shut!"

He and Bhooto turned away then, but not before the Colonel had snapped his fingers irritatedly at Matty and told him to stop eavesdropping and get on with his work.

Gary dug in his heels, his face flushed with anger. "That was a threat! He threatened me!"

"It certainly sounded that way," Bethan murmured.

"Oh Gary, why didn't you keep quiet?" Laura wailed. "Those two are dangerous. We'll have to keep well away from here from now on."

"No way!" Gary said, shaking his head defiantly. "He's up to something. And I'm going to find out what."

Bethan looked horrified. "You've got to be joking, Gary. Laura's right – they're dangerous. We shouldn't have anything to do with them."

"So we just let them carry on?"

"What else can we do?" Laura asked help-lessly.

"We could find out what he keeps in that bunker for a start," said Gary.

"How exactly?" Laura groaned. "It's locked. It's guarded by a pack of wild dogs and it's inside a three-metre-high fence."

Gary gave her a crooked little smile. "I'll give that some thought."

"Give it a *lot* of thought, Gary," Laura warned, turning towards home. "Because those two aren't playing games. Come on Beth, let's go home."

But Bethan hesitated. "Hang on ... look at Matty."

They glanced back.

Matty was standing at the fence. Hands gripping the wire netting. Peering out into the forest. The strangest look on his face. A look of longing – as if he was longing to be free and running wild through the forest instead of mending fences.

For a second, Laura thought he looked just like a caged wild animal himself.

Chapter 12

Snow was falling heavily again as they trudged homewards — drifting down through the tangle of branches, covering their earlier tracks. And the silence that came with it was eerie.

Gary and Bethan talked non-stop, but Laura felt on edge and couldn't help glancing over her shoulder every few seconds.

Nothing moved — except for the falling snow. Yet she had the strangest sensation that they weren't alone.

The wolf could sneak close under these conditions. He was perfectly camouflaged. His paws would be silent on the snow.

"Hurry up," she urged, practically walking

on her friends' heels, her skin prickling. He could be within attacking distance now. He could have picked up their scent, he could be licking his lips this very second. Wondering which of them would make the best meal.

"Can't you walk any faster?" she complained edgily.

"Not really," Bethan replied. "My boots keep slipping off in the snow."

Laura glanced back again. Something was following them. She could *feel* it.

At last they reached the edge of the forest and she breathed a sigh of relief. The wolf surely wouldn't follow them out into the open.

The lane was deserted. Everyone was indoors, keeping warm.

"You're quiet," Bethan remarked as they struggled through the deep snow in Coopers Lane.

"Am I?" Laura murmured, linking Bethan's arm for comfort.

"And you're jumpy. What's up?"

"I keep thinking we're being followed."

They all looked back, but there was nothing but a snowy country lane.

Gary shrugged. "It's that Colonel. He's enough to make anyone nervous. We've got to do something about him. If we could only find a way of getting into that bunker."

"It's impossible," Laura argued. "And it's dangerous. You can't mess about with people like that."

But Gary was determined. And they were still discussing the possibilities of finding out what he was up to, when they reached the main road.

"So, what now?" Bethan asked.

"I'm going to see Kess," said Gary. "Coming?"

Laura's hands and feet felt like blocks of ice, and as she considered the options of another cold walk to the vet's or going home and sitting in front of the fire, it happened!

The sensation of being followed was suddenly overpowering. They all spun round.

He was practically upon them. But it wasn't the wolf...

"Matty!"

He looked like a big walking snowman, with glowing cheeks and eyes that sparkled because of the snowflakes on his eyelashes.

"I scared you. I didn't mean to. Sorry."

"No, it's OK," Laura gasped, relieved that it wasn't the wolf. "Were you following us?"

He shuffled his feet. "Yeah. I just wondered if I could see them photos that you showed the Colonel."

"Of the wolf?" Laura asked, amazed that he'd followed them all this way just for that.

He gave a sort of disinterested shrug. "Well, it can't be a wolf, can it. There ain't none living wild. Only my mate's lost his dog – it looks a bit wolfish, and it's white. Thought it might be his."

Laura eyed him suspiciously. He looked nervous. "Yes, course you can see the pictures, Matty. Here you go."

He practically snatched the photos off her, and she studied him as he examined them closely.

"Yeah," he said at last. "This is my mate's dog all right. I'll tell him, thanks."

The others exchanged glances. Then Gary said, "Hate to tell you, only that's no dog. That's a wolf. We saw it close up."

Matty shook his head. "Nah! You're wrong. You wouldn't find a wolf round here. This is my mate's dog. I'd recognize it anywhere."

Laura had the strangest feeling that he was lying. He wasn't just mistaken – he was actually lying!

"What's your friend's name?" she asked, watching him carefully.

He hesitated just long enough for Laura to be positive he was making this story up. There was no friend, and no lost dog.

"Jim," he said a second later.

"And what's his dog's name?"

Matty swallowed hard. "Er ... Snowy, 'cos of his colour."

"Original," Gary murmured, not taken in by Matty's story either.

Matty seemed reluctant to hand the photos back. He clutched them to his chest as they chatted. "Sorry about your dog. Is she going to be all right?"

"She's going to be fine," Gary answered positively. Then his lip quivered. "I hope."

"She will be," Bethan reassured him. "She's being well looked after now." She glanced at

Matty. "Your sister is nursing her."

"Rachel? Good. She's really kind. She'll take care of your dog. Don't you worry."

"Matty," Laura said curiously. "Why was the Colonel so nasty to you? He said something about you knowing about wolves?"

Matty glanced away. "He sort of blames me, I suppose."

"Blames you for what?" Gary demanded.

"For that little wolf cub dying," he said simply.

"Why? What happened?" Bethan asked softly.

Matty took a deep breath. "Him and Bhooto brought a wolf cub back from Albania or somewhere. It was a beautiful little cub, pure white — and that's pretty rare. The Colonel wanted it specially..." He hesitated, as if wrestling with some secret thought. Then he continued. "It was my job to look after it. Bhooto wouldn't go near it. It spooked him out."

"I gather that. Do you know why?" Laura asked.

"He's superstitious," said Matty vaguely.

"Why? Are wolves bad luck or something?" Bethan remarked.

"Not as far as I know," Matty agreed. "Bhooto just had a *thing* about this little cub. Like he was scared of it. Like it would harm him."

"A little wolf cub!" Laura puzzled.

"Yeah," Matty continued. "I heard him talking to the Colonel one day. He said something like, it knows ... it knows. It ain't gonna forget. It's planning to get us when the time's right."

Laura frowned. "What did it know?"

Matty stared over their heads. "It ain't for me to say."

Gary was wildly curious. "Ah, come on, tell us. We *know* those two aren't what they pretend to be. So you can tell us."

But Matty shook his head. "I don't want to lose my job. Anyway, I don't *know* anything for sure... I've just got a feeling."

"A feeling about what?" Gary implored.

"I've got no proof," Matty answered, almost angrily. "I just overheard him once — talking about a collection..." His voice broke off and his eyes winced almost with pain. "Just forget it, will you."

"Tell us about the wolf cub," Laura interrupted softly, as Gary was about to try and prise more information from Matty.

His expression softened. "Ah, he was a great little cub. I really loved him – called him Flame because he was so fiery and brave. When the cub first arrived it wouldn't eat, wouldn't sleep. Just cowered in a corner and growled at everyone. Specially the Colonel and Bhooto."

"And you?" asked Bethan.

"Yeah, till it realized I wouldn't harm him. I used to sleep in his cage at nights. Let it cuddle up to me so it wasn't so scared."

"That's lovely," Laura murmured. "But what happened? The Colonel said…"

"It died!" Matty said simply, emotionlessly. "It just died. One morning I found it dead. I carried it in my arms up to the house to show them."

He held out his arms, so they could almost see that little wolf cub lying limp and lifeless…

"The Colonel went berserk," continued Matty. "Said it was my fault for not looking after it properly. I buried it in the forest."

"So why's Bhooto still spooked when anyone mentions wolf?" Gary puzzled.

Matty grinned suddenly. "He probably thinks it's a ghost wolf come to get him and the Colonel."

Laura stared at Matty. Something just didn't ring true ... but what? There was something not quite right here. Only she just couldn't put her finger on it.

Matty still seemed to be finding something amusing. "See Bhooto jump when you said you'd got a photo of the wolf? No wonder he's making me repair all the fences."

"Matty, it really was a wolf," Laura said seriously. "And it's a good idea to mend your fences. Because when we first saw the wolf, it was *inside* the park."

Matty's smile faltered. All kinds of emotions flashed across his face for a second. Confusion, joy, fear. Then slightly bemused he said, "You mean my mate's dog. It weren't a wolf."

"It was! We saw a wo—"

"You *saw*," Matty stated, his voice becoming hard, "a dog – just a big white dog. If anyone asks you, you tell them it was only a dog." His eyes became like pinpoints. "Specially if the Colonel asks you. Tell him it was a dog. You were mistaken. It wasn't a wolf."

Laura stared at him. What was this, another threat?

Then she saw beneath the grim expression, to his eyes. No, it wasn't a threat. She saw desperation there. He was pleading with them – begging them to say it was a dog, not a wolf.

But why?

Didn't he want it captured? Locked safely away where it couldn't harm anyone, or be harmed?

Her own eyes fluttered shut.

Here was someone else who refused to believe there was a wolf on the loose. Just what would it take to make people understand? Were they all waiting for someone to be attacked by the wolf before they'd believe?

She recalled those powerful jaws, those fierce fangs.

She shivered. Before long, someone was going to be attacked by that wolf.

Attacked ... or killed!

Chapter 13

"I'd better get back before they miss me," Matty said, handing the photographs back to Laura.

Gary nodded towards the pictures. "Laura took some better shots of the bunker, but the film got ruined. We're all intrigued by the Colonel's secret store room. What does he keep in there, anyway?"

Matty looked puzzled. "What store room?"

Gary pointed to the photo of the grassy mound in the enclosure. "This old military bunker."

Matty's eyes creased. "What bunker?"

"This hill," Laura explained. "The Colonel uses it as a store room."

Matty looked lost. "He stores things in a hill?"

Laura glanced at her friends. Then at Matty. "You didn't know?"

He scratched his head. "Know what?"

"This hill, Matty, it's really an underground bunker. They used them in the war. I think it was so enemy aircraft couldn't spot them."

His eyes widened. "Yeah?"

"You haven't a clue what we're on about, have you?" Gary exclaimed in disbelief.

"Nope."

"How long have you worked there?"

"About three years."

"And you've never seen him open up that bunker?" Laura asked in amazement.

"Suppose it's been open on my days off," Matty said simply. "Sometimes the Colonel can be OK. Sometimes he just comes up to me and the others and says, take tomorrow off – just like that. On the spur of the moment. And him and Bhooto do all the work for the day."

"How odd," Laura murmured. "The crates they unloaded looked really heavy. You'd think they'd want all the help they could get to unload them and store them away."

"It's obvious!" exclaimed Gary. "That creep doesn't want anyone knowing what he's doing. Not us, and not Matty or the others. And that's because he's doing something illegal!"

Clearly Matty had no idea what they were talking about, and he headed back to the park then, leaving them to walk to the vet's, Gary convinced more than ever now that the Colonel was up to something.

Turning the corner, a snowball hit Laura on the back of her head. She turned to find Nicholas, one of their classmates.

"Good shot hey?" he laughed. "This is great, isn't it."

"Great," she agreed with less enthusiasm than their freckled-faced friend. "How's your project going at the radio station?"

Nicholas groaned. "We've got to plan and write a ten minute documentary by tomorrow. We're going to broadcast it at midday."

Laura's eyes popped. "That's incredible! What a brilliant opportunity."

Nicholas just rolled his eyes upwards. "Yes,

well it would be if we could think of anything to do it on. Any ideas?"

"Sorry Nick," she replied, glancing at the others. "We've got enough problems at the moment."

Bethan smiled at him. "You'll think of something, I'm sure."

"You reckon?"

"Course you will. Anyway, we've got to go. See you."

They weren't allowed to see Kess straight away as the vet was examining her. They waited patiently outside the recovery room until he came out.

The kindly-faced vet ruffled Gary's hair. "Back again, lad? Good on you. Y'know, you might not think you're achieving anything, but believe me, your visits are doing Kess the world of good. Go on, in you go."

Kess was lying in her little compartment, her head resting sadly on her front paws. Her brown eyes glanced up as they came in, and for a brief second, she gave one very feeble wag of her tail.

"Did you see that?" Gary beamed, rushing

forward and opening up the cage front to pet her. "Hello girl, are you feeling better?"

Laura and Bethan made a fuss of her too, and were rewarded with another twitch of her golden tail, but then her eyes grew heavy and she slept.

"See what a little tender loving care can do?" said Rachel, bustling in to tidy the room.

Gary said nothing and Laura sensed that deep down he was really worried about Kess. Hoping to take his mind off things for a while she chatted to Rachel.

"We've just been talking to your brother. He was telling us about the little wolf cub he used to look after."

"Really?" Rachel murmured.

"It sounded like he really loved that cub."

"Must have been awful when it died," Bethan remarked.

Laura pulled a face at her. The last thing Gary would want to hear about was an animal dying. But Bethan seemed blissfully unaware that she might be upsetting him.

"It was," Rachel agreed, busying herself by tidying up the shelves.

"What did it die of?" Bethan asked.

"No one knows for sure," answered Rachel.

"Must have broken your brother's heart, when it died," Bethan went on. "I know how I'd feel."

"And me," Gary agreed, burying his face in Kess's fur.

Bethan bit her lip. "Oh … sorry."

Laura's gaze switched to Gary. Of course! That's what had seemed wrong when Matty told them about the cub.

He'd spoken with such emotion about the cub. Yet when he said it had died, he hadn't sounded the slightest bit upset. He'd been so matter-of-fact about it. As if he hadn't cared at all.

"*Did* it upset Matty when the cub died?" Laura asked Rachel, watching her carefully.

"Of course. He was dreadfully upset," Rachel answered, not glancing up.

"He said the Colonel blamed him for its death."

"Well, who else would he blame?" the nurse dismissed. "Him and Bhooto went nowhere near it."

"Bhooto's superstitious," Gary remarked. "You should have seen him jump when we showed them the photos we took of the wolf."

Rachel had been washing a metal food tray. It suddenly fell, clattering noisily on to the floor. "You … you couldn't have taken photos of the wolf – it died!" she blurted out.

Bethan's eyes widened. "Er, we're not talking about a ghost wolf here, are we by any chance?"

Rachel blustered about, opening cage doors, shutting them again. "I haven't a clue what we're talking about," she said brusquely. "The only wolf I knew died when it was a cub, about a year ago."

Laura frowned. "Well, obviously it can't be the same wolf. It must be a wild wolf. Only no one wants to believe us. The Colonel refused to believe we'd seen a wolf, even when we showed him our photos."

"You showed the Colonel…" Rachel murmured, the colour draining from her cheeks. "What did he say?"

"He said it was a dog," Laura replied, wondering why Rachel was getting so upset.

"And Matty ... what about him?"

"He said it was his friend's lost dog."

Rachel's eyes fluttered shut briefly. "Of course! That's what it is," she said, relieved. "Matty's friend's dog. I remember him telling me about it."

"Rebel?" Laura suggested. "John's dog?"

"Yes, Rebel!" Rachel exclaimed. "That dog looks so much like a wolf it's unbelievable."

Laura and her friends exchanged glances.

Rachel heaved a sigh, her colour returning. "That's sorted then. Oh, and I shouldn't mention it to the Colonel or Bhooto again. Just let it drop. I'll tell John that his dog's been seen. He can come and look for it."

With a brief smile, the nurse hurried out of the room.

Laura, Bethan and Gary just looked at each other.

Laura was the first to break the silence.

She ran her fingers raggedly back through her hair. "Why?" she exclaimed, frowning. "Why is everyone lying?"

Chapter 14

"Maybe Rachel just made a mistake," Bethan suggested as they huddled beside Kess's bed. "John, instead of Jim — it's a bit similar."

"And Rebel is similar to Snowy?" Laura exclaimed. "I could just as easily have called it Fido or Rover."

"So what does it all mean?" Gary groaned.

"It means," said Laura quietly, "that there is no Jim or John. There's no Snowy, Rebel or any other lost dog. We're talking about a wolf. We know it, Matty knows it, his sister and Bhooto all know it. The only one who really thinks it's a dog is the Colonel!"

"So we've got to convince him," said Bethan innocently.

Laura and Gary almost jumped on her.

"Bethan!" Gary raged. "Haven't you heard a word that's been said? Practically everyone is telling us not to talk about it to the Colonel."

"Well, I don't see why not," Bethan mumbled sulkily.

"Look," explained Gary. "I trust Rachel and Matty more than I trust the Colonel. Maybe they know something we don't. Anyway, there's no way I'm going back to that park unless it's to get a sneak look into the bunker."

"And that's not very likely, is it," Laura said flatly.

Gary raised his eyebrows mysteriously. "Well, actually, I've been thinking."

Laura folded her arms. "Go on … let's hear it."

His eyes sparkled suddenly. "Right! What we do is wait until there's another delivery. Then we sneak on to the lorry, it takes us past the African wild dogs, right up to the bunker. And while we're on the lorry, we look inside the crates and see what he's up to."

Laura would have laughed if it wasn't so serious. "Gary, you're not the invisible man. The Colonel will see you."

"Not if I'm careful."

"It won't work. Besides, we don't know when the next delivery will be. Could be weeks or even months."

Gary scratched his head. "We've got one clue."

"Which is?"

"Matty's never seen the bunker open, so the deliveries must come when all the workers are given the day off together." Gary pulled a face then. "Only that doesn't help us either, because we don't know when their next day off will be."

Laura thought for a moment. "Hang on..."

She dashed through to reception.

"Rachel..."

The nurse glanced up, frowning.

"I wanted to speak to Matty again about the animals at the park – for our project."

Her frown dissolved. "No problem. I'll have a word with him."

"Thing is, I don't like to bother him while

he's working. If I left you my phone number, would you ask him to ring me when he's going to have a day off. I'd need to know the day before…"

"Yes, sure. Jot it down," Rachel said, pushing a pen and pad towards her. "But I know he's not working tomorrow. None of the park-hands are. The Colonel's given them all the day off."

"Tomorrow!"

Rachel's eyes were cold. "That's right. I suppose the Colonel does have his good points occasionally."

"Thanks," Laura murmured. "Thanks a lot."

She dashed back to join the others, excitement gurgling in the pit of her stomach.

But if she could have seen into the future, it wouldn't have been excitement she felt.

It would have been fear.

Chapter 15

They met at Laura's house early next morning. Unsure of what they'd need, Laura had taken her camera, Gary had brought a torch and a screwdriver, and Bethan had brought chocolate in case they got hungry.

At seven thirty on a frosty winter's morning, it was barely light. The sky was an inky blue and as they trudged along, the ground crunched beneath their feet.

"We'd better check the bunker first," Gary suggested as they half walked, half slid, down Coopers Lane. "The next delivery might already be here."

Bethan peered out from beneath her scarf. "That's if there *is* a delivery today. Just because Matty's got the day off…"

"I know it's a long shot," Gary agreed. "But it's all we've got to go on at the minute."

"I think we all need our heads examining," Bethan complained, shivering. "Just think, I could still be in my bed!"

Laura felt icy cold too, and she linked Bethan's arm for comfort. But it wasn't the weather that was making her cold. It was the fear of bumping into the wolf again … or the Colonel. She wasn't sure which one was worse!

"There is another way of knowing if there's been a lorry today. Instead of going through the forest," she said hopefully.

"How?" asked Gary.

"Tyre tracks in the snow."

Gary looked impressed. "Good thinking. But if there are tyre tracks, we move fast. Agreed?"

Laura and Bethan exchanged glances.

"I suppose so," Laura reluctantly agreed. "But we're not taking unnecessary risks. I dread to think what the Colonel would do if he catches us trespassing."

A muffled wail came from beneath Bethan's

scarf. "I want my bed! This is dangerous and stupid!"

But Gary marched on. "He's a crook, and we're going to prove it." He glanced back at the girls. There was a determined look on his face. "We've got to — for Kess."

They trudged on in silence. And reaching the park they saw that nothing had disturbed the snow that morning. The road running past the park and forest showed that nothing had travelled that way since the last fall of snow the previous night.

Gary looked delighted. "Great. No deliveries yet."

"There probably won't even be one," Bethan grumbled. "Specially in this weather."

"We'll just have to wait and see," murmured Gary, glancing all around. Then suddenly he headed off towards the forest.

"Gary!" Bethan hissed.

He beckoned them over. "We can't just stand in the road. We've got to get out of sight."

Grumbling, the girls ran after him.

"I'm not going far into the forest," Laura told him, glancing around nervously.

"This will do," he said, crouching behind some bushes, close to the edge, with a clear view of any traffic approaching.

Laura and Bethan huddled down beside him. They were sheltered here. But still the wind whistled through the stark bare branches.

It was an eerie sound. Disturbing. Haunting.

"This is a terrible idea," Bethan complained after a few minutes. "What are we supposed to do? Sit here all day, freezing to death? I bet you there's no delivery today. The weather's too awful for one thing. And I think you're just imagining the Colonel's up to something."

"There'll be a delivery all right," Gary whispered confidently. "Why else would he give everyone the day off? Matty's supposed to be mending fences, remember?"

Laura felt too nervous to argue. Her stomach felt like it was tied into a knot.

The wolf could be anywhere. It might already have picked up their scent. She could imagine it – creeping towards them, flat on its stomach. Amber eyes burning into the backs of their heads. Saliva dribbling over its fangs.

It would keep low, out of sight – until the very last second. Then it would pounce…

"Look…!"

Laura shrieked and went to run, but Gary grabbed her and pulled her back.

"Keep down, there's a lorry coming."

"Oh! For heaven's sake, you scared me to death!" she gasped, her heart thudding. "I nearly had heart failure!"

Two lights were approaching along the road.

They crouched lower behind the bushes as the headlights cut through the pale light of morning. The vehicle moved painfully slowly, its engine growling as it struggled through the snow.

It came closer, then they saw the big shovel on the front as it cut a wide groove in the snow.

"Snow plough," Gary murmured gloomily as it grumbled by, and continued on its way.

They settled down again behind the bushes. Bethan shared out the chocolate, and Laura tried to stop her hands and feet from turning blue as they waited, and waited.

Slowly the frosty mist of morning lifted, and a bright winter sun cast warming rays over the forest.

"We can't stay here all day, I'm numb!" Bethan complained.

"Me too," Laura agreed, on the point of giving up and going home.

"You two go then," said Gary. "I'll... Hang on. Something's coming."

They huddled down behind the bush, and peered through the frosty branches to the end of the road.

A lorry trundled into view, travelling slowly, its wheels crunching in the snow.

Gary's eye sparkled. "This could be it!"

"I want to go home," Bethan wailed.

"Sshhush!" hissed Gary.

Scarcely daring to breathe, they waited and watched as the lorry skidded its way up the road. It was an old lorry with tarpaulin sides and just one driver.

As it neared, its indicator flashed and it turned into the driveway of the rare breeds park.

"Yes!" Gary breathed, punching the air.

"Right! Now it's going to have to stop at the gates till someone opens up. Are you ready?"

"Ready for what?" Bethan asked in a frightened voice.

Laura stared at him. "Gary, you're not really going to get in the lorry, are you?"

"Sure…"

Bethan backed away. "I can't… I'm sorry, I just can't!"

"Wait here then," Gary said quickly. "That's best anyway. If I don't come out, you two can get help."

"You're not going in on your own," Laura told him. "I'm coming too."

Gary looked steadily at her, as the lorry growled to a halt. "Are you sure?"

She nodded.

"Be careful," Bethan whispered.

"Now!" Gary hissed, darting from their hiding place and running to the back of the lorry.

He was up in a flash. One foot on the bumper, the next on a girder, and he dipped under the tarpaulin flap out of sight.

A second later he peeped out. "Coming?"

With one last glance at Bethan, Laura followed him, her camera bag feeling bulky and cumbersome as she scrambled frantically up into the lorry, terrified she'd feel the Colonel's hand on her collar at any moment.

Gary finally dragged her in.

For a few seconds Laura lay breathless. It was pitch black, and her heart was drumming a furious tune against her ribcage.

"You OK?" Gary whispered.

"Think so."

There was a click. His torch light cut through the gloom. He grinned. "We're in!"

"Yes, we're definitely in," Laura murmured, as fear folded itself around her, colder than the snow outside.

They were in.

In the lorry. About to go *in* the park. But she had the awful feeling that they were also *in* something else…

In terrible danger!

Chapter 16

It was icy cold beneath the tarpaulin. It smelt of damp wood – and something else.

"What's that smell?" she whispered.

"Your socks?"

"Gary! This is no time for jokes. What is that smell, it's sort of animally. Oh! You don't think…"

"What?"

"You don't think there's wild animals in here, do you?"

Gary shone the torch around the lorry. The thin pale beam picked out six large wooden crates. "Don't know… In there, maybe. Here, hold the torch," he instructed, getting his screwdriver out.

"What are you doing?"

"Gonna look inside. How else are we going to find out?" he said, pushing the screwdriver beneath one of the planks.

"But there might be an animal in there," Laura gasped, horrified. "That smell – it's really odd."

"Can't hear any growling or scuffling – I don't think there's any animals. Anyway, they wouldn't transport animals in this type of crate. Let's have a look anyway."

Surprisingly, the plank of wood levered up easily. Gary shone his torch in.

"What's in there?" Laura hissed. "What can you see?"

"Not much, a load of straw..." He stretched over the crate and delved about inside.

"Gary, be careful!" Laura cried, horrified. "There might be snakes or anything."

"Can't feel anything." He re-emerged looking puzzled. "Not a thing. It's nothing but straw."

"Foodstuffs, just like the Colonel said," Laura murmured, disappointed.

"No! I don't believe it!" Gary quietly raged.

And to Laura's horror he lowered himself completely into the crate for a closer inspection.

"Gary!"

He disappeared under the pile of straw, then re-appeared a few moments later, practically spitting the stuff.

"I don't believe this. Let's look in another crate."

He climbed out just as the lorry lurched forward.

Their eyes met. Nervously he said, "Well there's no going back now!"

Laura peeped out from under the tarpaulin just in time to see Bhooto padlocking the gates after them. A moment later he was joined by the Colonel.

The two men followed the lorry. Talking quietly. Looking edgy.

Keeping a sharp lookout, Laura thought.

As they headed towards the animal enclosures, Bhooto went into a shed and came out with a thick plastic bag full of chunks of meat.

Laura glanced at Gary. He was struggling

to keep his balance in the moving lorry. Even the crates were wobbling around.

"This is it, Gary. He's got the meat to distract those African wild dogs. Whatever's in these crates, it's heading for his secret bunker."

Gary was levering another crate open. "There's got to be something here. No one goes to all this trouble for a load of old hay."

"Hurry Gary. We'll be at the wild dogs' enclosure in a minute."

"Straw again!" he muttered, hanging on to the crate as it rocked about in the lorry.

"Gary…"

"What?"

"There could be something in one of those," Laura murmured, pointing to two crates at the front end of the lorry. "There must be something heavy in them. They aren't rocking about like the others."

Gary gave them a push. They didn't budge.

Laura scrambled forward. "The others with straw in could be decoys, in case they get stopped by the police."

"So you *do* think he's up to something dodgy!" Gary exclaimed.

She shrugged helplessly. "There's only one way to find out. But you'll have to be quick."

Taking a deep breath, he got to work with his screwdriver. "This one's nailed down a lot harder than the others."

"Keep trying," she breathed, as the lorry lurched to a stop again.

Outside, Bhooto began shouting at the wild dogs to go get their breakfasts.

Laura peered out. They were outside the enclosure. The pointed-eared dogs were in a far corner, feasting on the meat Bhooto had thrown them.

The lorry moved forward. Into the enclosure. Bhooto slammed the gate shut.

Laura's throat tightened. In a few seconds the Colonel was going to open up the lorry!

Suddenly, the contents of the crates didn't seem important. If they were discovered now there was no saying what he would do.

If this was part of an illegal trade, it was obviously one that made him very rich.

And was he going to take kindly to two kids messing everything up for him?

Somehow she didn't think so.

Chapter 17

"Got it!" Gary exclaimed, managing to ease a slat of wood up without making too much noise.

Laura shone the torch into the crate as a waft of animal scent drifted out.

"What on earth are they?" she puzzled, as the torch light picked out some large curved grey cone-shaped objects.

Gary's eyes narrowed as he reached in to touch them. And then a look of absolute horror creased his face. "Oh no!" he breathed. "It can't be!"

"What is it ... Gary, tell me!"

"You tell me," he whispered. "Tell me I'm wrong – please..."

Swallowing hard, Laura reached into the crate. A sharp, hard point stuck into her hand. She felt the strange rough-smooth texture of the objects. Faintly ribbed. Hard – like horn...

She blinked. "Horns?" she whispered in disbelief.

Gary nodded. "Rhino horns!"

Her mouth dropped open. "Rhino horns!" They've killed rhinos just to get their horns – that's terrible!"

But there was no time to take in the full horror of their discovery. The Colonel and Bhooto were at the back of the lorry.

"We've got to hide!" Laura breathed. "Quick, in that crate of straw."

Within seconds they'd both squeezed into the crate. Laura placed the wooden planks back over the hole and prayed the Colonel wouldn't notice.

A moment later the tarpaulin was lifted. Bright winter sunlight streaked through the cracks in their crate. The lorry shook as the two men jumped on board.

"Which ones is it?" Bhooto asked, standing

so close that Laura could see the snow on his boots.

The Colonel gave the crate next to theirs a shove. "Not that one, too light."

Laura crouched rigid, afraid even to breathe. Only her eyes moved, darting towards Gary, finding him looking as tense as her.

If they shook this crate, the game would be up. It would feel heavy with them inside. Heavy enough for the Colonel to investigate...

"Ah ha! There's my babies!" the Colonel suddenly said, striding towards the far end of the lorry.

Laura's eyes fluttered shut in relief as his boots thudded past – centimetres from where they sat huddled. Moments later there was the sound of cracking wood as he levered more planks off the crate. Then he laughed in sheer delight.

"Look at this Bhooto, just look at it. What a beautiful sight. It gets better and better."

"It sure does," Bhooto agreed.

"Right, let's get them unloaded."

Through the cracks in their crate Laura saw a fork-lift truck suddenly appear at the back of the lorry, driven, she guessed, by the lorry driver. The long metal forks pushed forward into the lorry. But to her horror they slid right under the crate they were in.

"Not us, idiot!" Gary hissed as they were lifted upwards and outwards.

Laura clasped her hand over her mouth. It felt like a ride at the funfair, almost like flying.

But it was over in seconds. They were deposited on the ground, out of the way, while the fork-lift truck returned for the important crates.

"Do you think they'll put us back in the lorry, when they've got the horns out?" Laura murmured anxiously.

"I think I'd prefer to take my chances with the wild dogs," Gary muttered angrily. "Rhino horn – that's diabolical!"

The Colonel shouted to the driver to give them a hand with a crate. He did as he was told. And while they were busy, Laura and Gary peered out to find themselves staring directly into the bunker.

It was a long shadowy room, like a big underground warehouse, lined from one end to the other with crates – just like the two inside the lorry.

They looked at each other in horror.

"All full of rhino horns…" Laura murmured. "Oh Gary, just think how many deaths they're responsible for. It's terrible. Why have they done it?"

"Rhino horn is valuable," Gary explained. "It's ground up and exported to places like China. They put it into aphrodisiacs and medicines. I saw a TV programme about it. This lot must be worth hundreds of thousands of pounds. Millions even maybe."

"And it's illegal?" Laura asked, already knowing the answer.

"*Very!* Not to mention what he's doing to the rhinoceros population." His eyes blazed. "Some animal lover! I knew it. I knew it all along." He got to his feet. "Come on…"

"What are you doing?" Laura gasped.

"We're going to take photos, quick while they're still in the lorry."

Before she could argue, Gary had squeezed up and out of the crate. Panic-stricken, Laura followed.

They crouched down by the lorry wheels. With trembling hands, Laura took picture after picture of the bunker.

"Wish we could photograph the actual horns," Gary complained.

"We can't. This will have to do."

Suddenly the driver jumped down from the lorry and got into the fork-lift truck. He began manoeuvring the forks until they were beneath the heavy crate.

"Easy does it," warned the Colonel. "Steady now. Be careful man... Watch out, it's overbalancing!"

Too late. The crate toppled sideways, crashing to the ground. Splintering the wood and scattering a half dozen rhino horns into the snow.

Laura moved swiftly. Capturing the tangle of rhino horn, splintered wood – and the lorry's registration number – on film.

"Hey!" someone bellowed.

They glanced up into the startled driver's face. "What! What the dickens... Colonel! Colonel! There's two kids here!"

"Run!" Gary yelled, grabbing Laura's arm

and dragging her across the animal enclosure.

They practically flew across the open ground. Behind them came furious shouts as the Colonel and Bhooto looked out from the lorry.

"Stop them!" the Colonel bellowed. "They can't get away. You two, come back – now!"

Laura and Gary fled. Feet barely touching the snow. Skidding and racing towards the gate.

The sudden noise and commotion startled the wild dogs and, taking fright, they scattered in all directions.

Laura screamed as they darted around, teeth bared ready to defend themselves if they had to.

"Ignore them," Gary gasped. "Just keep running."

Behind, more dangerous than any wild animal, the three men gave chase.

"Don't stop," Gary panted. "They'll kill us if they catch us."

Laura felt as if her lungs were bursting as they raced towards the gate. "The gate's shut!"

Of course she knew that. She'd seen Bhooto shut it – but had he padlocked it?

She couldn't remember.

Please, don't let it be locked, she prayed as they raced towards it.

"Faster, Laura, faster!"

Please... please... don't be locked...

Bhooto was gaining on them. She could hear his heavy boots thudding through the snow, close behind. If it was padlocked there was no escape. They were trapped.

And as good as dead!

Chapter 18

The padlock dangled from a bar across the gate. They skidded to a halt.

"Gary, is it locked? Oh, God, I hope not!" Laura cried, glancing back frantically, just in time to see Bhooto stumble headlong into the snow as one of the strange-looking dogs darted in between his legs, tripping him up.

Suddenly the gate was open.

Gary whooped with joy. "He didn't lock it. Can you believe that!"

"Quick!" Laura ordered, and they dived through, banging it shut behind them, and clicking the padlock into place.

Two seconds later, Bhooto crashed into the

fence. Eyes bulging with rage, he shook the gate until it looked ready to fall off its hinges.

Laura stood, transfixed with terror, staring at the face on the other side of the cage. A face contorted with fury.

"Come on!" Gary gasped, grabbing Laura's arm and dragging her away.

They raced towards the exit, slithering and sliding in the snow. Glancing back, she saw the Colonel had reached the gate. And in between shooing the dogs away, as they regained their courage, he was fumbling with the gate key.

"They'll be out in a second," she cried. "Hurry, Gary, hurry!"

But the thick snow underfoot made running ten times more difficult. Their legs were like lead. Then, after turning a corner by the reptile house, they saw to their dismay that their exit was locked and bolted.

"It's all locked up!" Gary said, his mind working quickly. "It's too high to climb... Quick, this way."

They raced towards the gate marked private, which led through to the Colonel's house.

Suddenly Gary grabbed Laura's arm and dragged her back. "Hang on!"

"What?"

"They'll track us down — specially Bhooto…"

Laura spotted the big deep footprints that the Colonel and Bhooto had made earlier. "Step in their footprints!"

"Brilliant… Come on then."

Awkwardly they made their way across his garden, making sure they made no footprints of their own.

But even here, there was no escape. His home was like a fortress. There was no way through to the front of the house — and safety. Everywhere was barricaded with high walls and fences.

"Try his back door," Laura gasped, panting for breath. "We could run through his house and out the front."

"It'll be locked, it's bound to be," Gary wailed.

"Try it anyway," Laura urged frantically.

To their amazement, the door opened.

They stared at each other for a second, then

dashed inside. The warmth of the house made Laura's head spin, and she staggered a little.

"You OK?"

She nodded, clutching her side. Suddenly Gary pulled off his boots. Laura cast him a puzzled look.

"Take yours off, or we'll make footprints on the carpet."

"That's very considerate," Laura murmured.

Gary pulled a face. "I couldn't care less about his mouldy old carpet. I just don't want them to know we've been here."

"I know, I was joking."

"I'll laugh later, now let's get out of here."

They raced along the hallway, boots in hand, only to find that the front door refused to open.

"Oh no, it's one of those that need a key," Gary wailed. "Quick, see if you can see one anywhere."

Frantically, they searched, finding nothing. Until a noise from the rear of the house made their blood run cold.

Voices.

The Colonel and Bhooto.

"Get the rifle, Bhooto. They can't have gone far. They're not getting away. I'm not losing out on this deal now. No little kid's going to pull the plug on me. They're dead!"

Laura felt sick. That was no idle threat. The Colonel would have no worries about killing them.

Gary grabbed her sleeve. "Upstairs – quick!"

They tiptoed up, almost afraid to breathe. Up the thickly carpeted stairway to the very top of the house. Then silently along the corridor to the furthest room.

Downstairs the Colonel's voice boomed out in fury. "Check the house out first, Bhooto. You do upstairs, I'll do down. You never know…"

Laura grabbed Gary's arm, her eyes wide and frightened.

"Hide!" he whispered.

"Where?"

Gary turned a door handle. "This will have to do. Quick!"

Laura followed him in, her heart hammering.

The room was warm and smelt of cigar smoke – it smelt of the Colonel. Bookshelves lined the walls. There was a big heavy desk made of rich red mahogany and a leather-covered swivel chair. Filing cabinets, computer, telephone. Everything for the respectable businessman that he pretended to be.

The sound of Bhooto's heavy boots on the stairs made Laura's blood run cold.

"If he comes in here…"

Gary grabbed her arm. "Behind that cabinet… Look, there's a sort of alcove."

They darted behind the filing cabinet into a narrow recess in the wall and crouched down, squeezing themselves into the tiny space, praying that Bhooto would only glance in, because if he bothered to look behind the cabinet, they were done for.

Making themselves as small as possible, Laura accidentally pressed an electrical switch in the skirting board.

Just an ordinary switch…

But suddenly the wall they were leaning on

slid open and they toppled backwards into another room.

A secret room.

They scrambled to their knees, startled. Confused.

There was a similar switch on this side. Gary clicked it down and the door slid silently back into place. A moment later, they heard Bhooto enter the study. Laura closed her eyes in terror, listening as he searched the room they'd been in a second earlier.

And then to her relief she heard him leave. His feet clumped noisily back down the stairs as he called to the Colonel that they weren't there.

Only then, just as Laura began to breathe a sigh of relief, did she experience the awful sensation of being watched.

The hairs on the back of her neck began to prickle.

Afraid almost to look, she reached for Gary, then slowly, very slowly turned into the secret room.

Her knees buckled.

No wonder she thought she was being

watched. They *were* being watched. Dozens of pairs of eyes were staring down at them.

But staring blindly...

Helplessly, wordlessly, she and Gary looked up at the four walls that surrounded them.

It was an elegant room. Oak panelled walls, rich furniture. Heavy drapes at the small window.

But Laura felt sick to her stomach. For on each of the four walls, there hung the mounted heads of wild animals.

Elephant, lion, tiger, stag, zebra, bear... So many beautiful, tragic animals. Stuck up there as trophies.

And photographs too of the Colonel and Bhooto, proudly posing with some poor animal they'd shot.

The Colonel has a cruel streak.

Cruel wasn't the word for it.

He was evil!

And protector of wildlife?

He was nothing but a cold-blooded murderer.

"No rhino, you notice," Gary breathed, his face white with shock. "Suppose he couldn't have a rhino up there without its horns. And he has other uses for their horns."

Laura shivered violently.

Yes, collecting rhino horns was making the Colonel very rich. This was a very lucrative business he was involved in. He wasn't about to let a couple of kids ruin it for him.

She felt afraid – more afraid than she'd ever felt in her life. The Colonel and Bhooto were after them.

And great hunters, such as they obviously were, weren't likely to let them slip away.

They would be tracked down.

Now they were the prey, just like all these poor animals up on the walls. No doubt the Colonel wouldn't rest until he'd caught them...

A terrifying thought hit her.

When they were caught – would their heads be stuck up there on the wall too?

Like trophies?

Chapter 19

"He's a big game hunter!" Laura cried in horror. "He doesn't protect animals – he kills them, for sport."

"And for money," Gary reminded her – as if she needed reminding.

"Oh Gary, what are we going to do?"

His eyes blazed with anger. "We're going to tell everyone," he said fiercely. "We're gonna let everyone know that he's not Mister Wonderful at all. He's an animal killer. And I'm going to tell the whole world."

"Ring the police," Laura said, clicking the switch which opened the secret door into the Colonel's study. She ran to the telephone.

She'd dialled the first two nines before realizing the line was dead.

"Oh no! He must have disconnected it, just in case."

A sound from outside made Gary rush to the window which looked down on to the road. "They're out the front," he whispered.

Laura peered over his shoulder, keeping well back in case they glanced up and spotted them. The Colonel and Bhooto had just opened the gates to let the lorry out. It roared away down the road, wheels spinning in the snow.

The Colonel and Bhooto, with a shotgun under his arm, remained in the driveway. Standing guard.

"Right," said Gary determinedly. "While they're at the front, we'll double back through the park. There must be holes in the fence. If we get into the forest, they'll never find us."

"Come on then!" Laura said, dragging him.

They moved swiftly, racing down the stairs and out through the back, pulling on their boots as they ran. There was no time now to worry about leaving footprints in the snow, and they ran as fast as they could.

Across the Colonel's garden, out through his gate and into the park again. Running, slithering and sliding they raced past the reptile house and the African wild dog enclosure and the Arctic foxes and the monkey house. Past the aviaries and up towards the perimeter fence.

"I can't, Gary," Laura gasped, as the stitch in her side bent her double. "I can't…"

"Rest a minute then," he said. "I'll try and find some way out. There must be a hole somewhere – the wolf found it."

"Maybe Matty's already mended it," Laura gasped anxiously.

Gary looked afraid suddenly. "Don't say that."

Laura stood, clutching her side as Gary clambered up the embankment to the fence that encircled the park. He was some way off when he waved and shouted.

"Found one!"

She stumbled towards him, struggling up the embankment to the fencing. Gary reached down and hauled her up.

"Nearly didn't spot it with all this snow," he said, pulling up a piece of netting. "It's not very big either, but we should be able to squeeze under — just. Go on. You first while I hold it up."

On hands and knees in the snow, dragging her camera behind her, Laura crawled beneath the fence. Then she held the netting up for Gary, and he scrambled through after her.

"We're free!" he grinned.

But Laura found nothing to smile about. On one side of the fence lived the worst villain she'd ever known in her life. And on this side, there roamed a wolf.

She didn't know which was the most dangerous.

Chapter 20

Keeping close to the trees at the side of the fence, they hurried through the forest. The sun was up now, sending a dazzling winter sunlight to warm their backs as they trudged through the snow.

Glancing back, it was impossible to make out anything except a bright shimmering haze. But in front, everything was clear. Crystal clear...

So clear that there was no mistaking the Colonel and Bhooto in the distance – and heading their way.

"Quick!" Gary hissed, grabbing Laura's arm and dragging her deeper into the forest.

"Do you think they saw us?" breathed Laura.

"I don't think so. The sun's in their eyes looking this way."

"What are we going to do?"

"We'd better get well away from the path," said Gary, leading her towards the heart of the forest. "Come on. And keep your head down."

Darting from tree to tree, hiding behind bushes and shrubs, they got as far away from the Colonel and his accomplice as they could.

"I'd no idea the forest was this big," Laura said nervously. "We're not going to get lost or anything, are we?"

"Course not. The sun rises in the east and it was directly behind us. We know the way home is west, so once we're well away from those two, we simply head west. We'll come out near Coopers Lane."

Laura cast him a crooked little smile. "Let's hope the sun doesn't go in then."

There was less snow underfoot as they walked deeper into the forest. The branches overhead tangled together forming a dark canopy, protecting the undergrowth from the worst of the snow. But it also blocked out the light and the warmth from the sun. Now it was bitterly cold and dark.

"Gary… we can't see the sun any more," Laura warned unhappily.

"It doesn't matter yet. The main thing is to get well away from the Colonel first. Then we head west."

"And west is that way?" she asked, pointing to her right.

"Correct!"

She breathed a sigh of relief and trudged on. All around, everything was silent and still, the only noise being the sudden clapping of wings as a wood pigeon took fright.

"Oh! I've just thought of something," Laura said anxiously.

"What?"

She stared at him. "Bethan! She'll be frantic."

"Nah," Gary said uneasily. "She'll be OK."

"I don't think so," Laura fretted. "If she was still hiding when the lorry drove off, she won't know if we were in it or not. And what if the Colonel saw her… Oh God, Gary. What do you think he'd do?"

"Stop worrying. It's us he's after," Gary replied. But the look on his face was grim.

Laura suddenly felt like crying. "We should never have got involved in this. They're real villains. They're evil. They kill things for fun. I don't suppose they care any more about kids than animals."

"Calm down Laura, we're going to be OK. Look, I reckon we've gone far enough this way. We'll head west now."

They turned to the right, weaving a path between the tangle of bracken and shrubbery, avoiding the squelchy, marshy patches that had frozen into icy puddles.

"We're going the wrong way!" Laura cried suddenly.

"No we're not."

"We are," she argued, panic welling up inside her. "This doesn't feel right."

Gary frowned and his eyes narrowed. "No, we're heading the right way. Trust me. Look, there's a bright bit by that clearing ahead. We'll get our bearings from there."

They quickened their pace. Walking briskly towards the patch of sunlight, reaching it,

Laura looked up. Above was a patch of grey-white sky. Nothing more, nothing less.

No magic compass saying north, south, east and west.

"It's this way, I'm positive," Gary said before she could utter a word.

Laura silently followed him, feeling less and less confident.

For all they knew, they could be heading straight back the way they'd come.

Straight back towards the Colonel!

Chapter 21

"I don't like this, Gary," Laura murmured anxiously. "We've been walking for ages. We should have reached the road by now."

"It can't be much further," Gary replied, glancing this way and that, a worried look on his face.

The forest seemed to be closing in on them. Branches that had bowed beneath the weight of snow now barred their way. If there was a pathway it was well hidden beneath bracken and dead leaves and more snow.

"Admit it Gary, we're lost..." Laura began, then something caught her eye. Far off in the distance – a figure.

"Who's that?" she breathed, her heart

thumping wildly.

Gary pulled her out of sight, ducking down behind a gnarled old elm tree. Cautiously they peered around it.

"It's Matty!" she exclaimed, never more relieved in the whole of her life to see someone. She jumped up and went to shout at the top of her voice. Gary yanked her back.

"Sshhh!"

"What?" she cried, stumbling backwards to land in a heap on the ground.

Gary crouched down beside her. "Your voice will carry. The Colonel's bound to hear."

"But Matty could help us," she wailed, close to tears again.

"I know that. And we'll catch him up. But we've got to do it quietly." He cast her a hopeful smile and dusted the snow off her coat. "It'll be all right you know, don't worry."

"You think so?" she murmured doubtfully.

"Course. Now come on."

They set off in Matty's direction. Only in that few moments, he had vanished from sight in the dense undergrowth.

"He's gone!" Laura cried. "Oh Gary, you should have let me shout to him."

"He can't have gone far…" His words died on his lips. His face paled and his mouth dropped open.

Laura screamed. And for what seemed an eternity, her scream echoed around and around the tree tops before drifting far off into the distance.

The wolf!

It stood not ten paces away from them, its ears twitching at the sound of Laura's scream.

A terrifying sight – yet beautiful, with its thick white fur coat and clear amber eyes that regarded them with curiosity.

"Don't make any sudden movements," Gary whispered, holding on to Laura's sleeve and edging backwards. "Move slowly, don't show it you're afraid."

"But I am…"

"It might be more scared of us."

"Some hope!"

Inch by inch, they backed away from the ferocious animal. Twigs cracked underfoot. Branches scratched the backs of their heads as they stared unblinking at the wolf as they made their get-away.

Almost afraid to breathe, they slowly moved away from the wolf. Further ... further ... almost out of its sight...

It didn't seem to want to pursue them. It stayed amongst the trees and undergrowth until at last they couldn't see it. And it couldn't see them.

"Run!" Gary hissed. "Run!"

They turned quickly and started to sprint away.

But two powerful figures had loomed up out of nowhere. Blocking the light.

Blocking their escape.

There was no chance to stop. Strong arms seized them instantly. Laura screamed again. Gary went crazy, arms and feet punching and kicking.

But it was useless.

The hunt was over. The prey had been captured by the predators – the Colonel and Bhooto.

And there was no escape.

Chapter 22

"Now, what shall we do with these two little prizes, Bhooto my friend?" the Colonel sneered unpleasantly.

Bhooto, with his gun poised, grinned callously. "We could feed them to the wild dogs. They'd enjoy some nice tender fresh meat."

"Let go of us!" Laura shouted.

"But my dear, how can we?" the Colonel said, pretending to be sad. "You know far too much. You've discovered our little importing and exporting business. And somehow I don't think you could be trusted to keep it to yourself. Do you?"

"We would, honestly," Laura lied. "We won't say a word."

The Colonel smiled an unpleasant smile. "Now why don't I believe you?"

"But you can trust us," Laura promised. "Just let us go. Please!"

"I don't think so," remarked the Colonel. "Now I think we'll finish this conversation back at the house, where it's a little warmer. Bhooto's trigger finger seems to be freezing. I should hate it to go so numb that he might accidentally pull the trigger – specially when the gun's pointing straight at you." He smiled again. "Now shall we go?"

"Do as he says, Gary," Laura murmured.

They walked back towards the house.

Nearing the road, the Colonel went ahead to check there was no one around who could witness what was going on.

The road was clear and he gestured for Bhooto to bring Laura and Gary quickly.

They glanced at the bush where they'd left Bethan hiding.

She wasn't there.

"Inside," the Colonel ordered, unlocking his wrought iron gates and ushering them up to his front door, no longer bothering to turn on the charm.

"What are you going to do with us?" Gary demanded.

"We're going to feed you to the wild dogs! Now shut up. I've got to think," he snapped, bundling them into his house and kicking the door shut behind them. "Bhooto, take them upstairs. I'm going to have to make some quick arrangements to ship all the horns out before schedule."

"OK. You two – upstairs!"

With the barrel of the gun poking into their backs, they had no choice but to go up.

A couple of steps ahead of Bhooto, Gary whispered in Laura's ear.

"I could try and kick the gun out of his hand. We could make a run for it. The Colonel didn't lock his front door."

"No! It's too risky," Laura whispered. "You wouldn't be able to, he's too strong."

"Hey! Stop your whispering!" Bhooto bellowed suddenly, making them both jump.

They climbed to the top of the house and along to the furthest room, where they had hidden earlier.

Laura's blood ran cold.

"Oh God!" she breathed, feeling faint.

"What?" Gary murmured.

She gulped. "They're going to add our heads to their collection. I know they are."

Bhooto must have overheard. "So that's where you were hiding – in the trophy room! Well that's right. We're gonna slice 'em right off from here..." and still grinning, he ran his finger menacingly across his throat.

"Take no notice," Gary remarked. "He's just trying to scare us."

"It's working," Laura admitted shakily.

They went into the Colonel's study, and with a big wide grin on his face, Bhooto flicked the switch in the alcove. The secret door slid open.

"In you go. You may as well admire the collection before you become part of it yourselves!"

He started laughing. A horrible gravelly laugh.

Laura and Gary turned away. Laura looked up at all the poor dead animals, disgusted that so many beautiful creatures had been killed just for sport.

"How could you?" she murmured, gazing sadly at the large head of a tiger high above the fireplace.

Alive, the tiger must have been a magnificent animal. Its head was huge, and beautifully marked. Now in death its face was set in a permanently fierce growl, its jaws wide open, teeth bared.

How fierce and courageous it looked – and probably was. But it had been no match for two cold-hearted hunters armed with guns.

"You won't get away with this," Gary said angrily. "Our friend will have gone for the police by now. They'll be here any second."

"Who will?" snapped the Colonel as he strode into the room.

"The police. Our friend's gone to fetch them."

The Colonel smiled coldly. "Nice try, lad. But I don't believe you. Besides, you should be pleased with yourself for disrupting our organization here. I've had to put wheels in motion to get all those horns moved pretty quick."

Gary's eyes narrowed with hatred. "Yeah,

well, you're going to have to kill us to stop us telling."

"Gary!" Laura cried. "Shut up!"

The Colonel looked amused. "Do you know, I was about to suggest that without any evidence, it would be just your word against mine. But if you continue to annoy me, I might just follow Bhooto's suggestion and feed you to my wild dogs!"

Bhooto looked as if he would relish the idea. "And we can mount their heads up there. What do ya say?"

The Colonel chuckled and wandered over to the fireplace. "Yes, what do you think of my little collection? We have had some fun over the years, haven't we, Bhooto!"

"You're sick!" Laura cried furiously. "You're sick and vile and…"

She didn't get the last word out. A sudden flash of pure white leapt through the open door.

The wolf!

Teeth bared, it sprang straight at Bhooto, closing its powerful jaws around his arm and flattening him to the floor.

161

In that instant, Bhooto's face registered all the terror that these poor dead animals must have felt before they were killed.

In fright his finger tightened around the trigger of his gun. There was an almighty explosion.

Laura and Gary ducked automatically.

The bullet whizzed through the air and hit the wall above the fireplace – above the Colonel.

It sliced straight through the hook that supported the tiger's head.

Laura thought afterwards that she'd heard a ghostly roar of triumph, but right then, all she was aware of was the huge open-mouthed tiger's head falling down from the wall.

Straight down – to land on top of the Colonel!

His own head disappeared instantly inside the tiger's jaws and his legs buckled under the impact and weight.

Laura and Gary could only stare at each other. Then in awed silence they peered down – first at the Colonel lying unconscious, with his head in the tiger's mouth. And then at Bhooto, lying there, quivering with terror as the one thing he was afraid of – the white wolf – stood guard over him. Its fangs bared, snarling and growling menacingly if he should even move.

Laura felt a gurgle of laughter bubble up inside her. "The animals – they've got their revenge!"

Gary shook his head in astonishment. "I don't know how or why that wolf followed us, but I'm sure glad he did."

"He came," said Matty suddenly, appearing as if by magic in the doorway, "because he had to avenge his family."

Matty came into the room, looking big and gangly with his long, fair hair clinging damply to his face. He looked down at Bhooto, then kicked the gun across the room, out of reach. Bhooto's eyes were popping. Whimpering and cringing, he begged Matty not to let the wolf tear him to shreds.

Ignoring Bhooto lying there looking pathetic now, Laura asked, "What do you mean – avenge his family?"

Matty's fists clenched. "These two creeps decided that what their collection of heads needed was a pure white wolf. They found a family of wolves with one of the cubs pure white."

"So they stole it?" Laura suggested.

Matty's face filled with rage. "Oh no. These two are too evil and cruel to just steal. They shot the others..." His voice trembled. "Killed them all, except for one. They brought him back here."

"How can you be sure?" Laura asked.

"I overheard them talking," said Matty. "And I knew it was true because of the way the cub acted towards them. Even when he was tiny, the way he looked at them – snarled and growled and spat whenever they came near. Oh, he was scared of them all right – terrified. But he never forgot what they did to his family. It was like he was saying, just you wait till I'm big, and then you'll be sorry."

"Do you think that's why Bhooto was so frightened of the wolf returning – even as a ghost? Because he thought it was coming to get revenge?" asked Laura.

Matty nodded. "I'm sure of it. Bhooto is superstitious about everything. He could handle a live wolf – so long as he'd got a gun. But the spirit of the wolf was something else."

Laura and Gary grinned at each other as they looked down at Bhooto still quivering with terror as the wolf remained coiled over him, its fangs, dripping saliva, centimetres from his petrified face.

"The Colonel didn't share Bhooto's fears then?" mused Laura.

"Nah, not him," Matty said. "He's too insensitive and smug to think anything could hurt him. Specially an animal."

"Well, an animal has certainly hurt him now!" grinned Gary as they glanced over at the Colonel, lying there with his head in the tiger's mouth.

Laura turned back to Matty. "But you said the wolf cub had died."

"I had to say that," Matty explained. "I overheard the Colonel telling Bhooto that once the cub grew to its full size they'd kill it for their collection." Matty's eyes glistened. "I couldn't let them do that!"

"You knew he was a big game hunter?" Gary asked. "You knew about all this?"

"I've never been in this room, but I knew it existed. I've overheard them talking – I might be dumb, but I'm not deaf!"

"You're not dumb!" Laura said outraged.

Matty simply shrugged and continued. "The only reason I didn't leave was because of the animals. I was scared they'd all end up like this ... and I just couldn't let them kill the wolf – Flame."

"Of course you couldn't," Laura murmured. "So what did you do?"

"My sister Rachel works at the vet's – you know that. Well, when I told her, she smuggled some drug out. I don't know what it was. Only that when she gave it to the cub, it knocked him so unconscious he looked dead. It didn't hurt him and he woke up later, just fine."

"But you said you'd buried him," said Laura, feeling the distinct urge to stroke the beautiful wolf, just as Matty was doing as he talked.

"Yeah, I said that. But really I took him home. Me and Rachel looked after him till he grew too big to keep."

"Then what did you do?" asked Gary.

"Rachel knew someone. He lives the other side of the moors. He has an animal sanctuary. We took him there." His face filled with love as he looked at the wolf. "But looks like he got out and came to look for me!"

"That's amazing," Laura murmured. "He found his way right back to you."

"Yeah, and you saw him first. When I heard you'd seen a wolf, I was dead scared the Colonel would guess what I'd done, and would hunt him down. That's why Rachel and me tried to convince you it was just a dog."

"Oh Matty, you could have told *us*," Laura said softly, unable to resist the urge to stroke the beautiful wolf any longer. Unafraid, she ran her fingers through its soft fur. "He must really love you, Matty."

He smiled. "Yeah, I reckon he does."

The sound of police sirens echoed suddenly outside. The noise became louder, followed by the sound of cars screaming to a halt. Car doors slamming and big heavy boots clumping up the stairs.

"The police – how?" exclaimed Laura, puzzled but infinitely relieved.

Matty looked relieved too, especially as the Colonel was beginning to come round. "Your friend must have gone to the police after all."

"Bethan?"

Matty nodded. "Yeah, I saw her near the forest earlier. I thought I'd spend my day off looking for Flame. I bumped into your friend. She told me what you were up to. I said if she was worried, she should tell the police."

"Looks like she did!" said Gary as six burly policemen hurtled into the room. They skidded to a halt at the sight that met their eyes.

The sergeant stepped forward. "Well now, I hope somone can explain exactly what's going on here!"

Laura and Gary beamed at each other. "With pleasure," Laura said happily.

But before they could begin, another officer – one with a look of terror on his face – interrupted. "Er, Sarge... I think I'd better warn you. That there is a wolf ... that's what that is. It's a bloomin' wolf!"

Laura, Gary and Matty looked at the officer innocently.

"A wolf!" Laura mocked. "You don't get wolves roaming free in this part of the world. Don't you know the difference between a wolf and a dog?" She shook her head in amazement. "Honestly, I'm surprised at you!"

Chapter 23

Handcuffed and held secure by four of the biggest policemen Laura had ever seen, the Colonel and Bhooto were made to hand over the keys to the bunker and watch as the police opened it up.

Matty was given the job of distracting the African wild dogs while the police went in. Calling each by its name he coaxed them into their den as the bunker doors were thrown wide.

Laura, with the wolf standing by her side like an obedient dog, looked at the two evil men. They didn't look so big and dangerous now. They looked defeated, broken. They stood with their heads hanging in shame as the police discovered their illegal trade.

"Their hunting days are well and truly over," the police sergeant eventually said, as he ordered them to be taken off to the police cells. "They're going to be locked away for a very long time!"

"Good!" both Laura and Gary agreed together.

The sergeant turned to Matty as he secured the wild dogs' enclosure again. "Will you be able to take care of this place until it gets a new owner?"

"Yeah, course. I always take good care of the animals," Matty replied. Then his face dropped. "Only what happens if it don't get a new owner? I ain't got enough money to pay for all their food and stuff."

The police sergeant shook his head. "I don't honestly know, son. You'll have to worry about that problem when it happens. Now, if I can leave you and your ... er ... pet dog in charge here, I'll run these two young heroes back home."

"We'll be back later," Laura promised. "We'll try and think of what we can do. Don't worry, Matty."

But Matty did look worried.

Sensing his concern, the wolf nuzzled its head into Matty's hand. He patted it affectionately, but in his eyes there was a look of real anxiety.

Laura and Gary had never been in a police car before. They sat quietly in the back, beginning to feel slightly shell-shocked after all that had gone on.

"There's Bethan!" Gary suddenly cried, spotting her talking to Nicholas in the street. "Sergeant, can you let us out here, please?"

"Here? You sure?"

"Positive. That's our friend, she'll have been worried about us."

"Righto," he said, drawing the car to a halt in the slushy gutter. "There you go then. Now we've got your addresses, someone will be around later for statements."

They clambered out of the car and called to Bethan. She gave a little shriek when she saw them, and flew at them, throwing her arms around each of their necks and hugging them fiercely.

172

"What happened to you? I've been frantic!"

"They've arrested the Colonel and Bhooto," Laura quickly explained. "Gary was right. They are crooks."

Bethan gasped. "Why ... what happened? Tell me!"

Laura took a deep breath. "It's a long story..."

Bethan and Nicholas listened, wide-eyed with astonishment, as Laura and Gary told them everything that had gone on. And finally, when the whole tale was told, Gary added, "The problem now is that Cottesbrook Rare Breeds Park desperately needs a new owner – and soon."

Nicholas's freckled face lit up. "Hey, you guys. I've just had a great idea."

The local radio station was bustling as their school friends crowded into the reception area ready to do their broadcast for their school project.

Nicholas gathered them around and quickly explained there had been a change of plan.

There was a much more important story that needed to be told.

The radio presenter was slick and handsome with a toothpaste smile and a chocolate-coated voice. He took Laura and Gary into a glass-walled studio. Sat them down in front of microphones and put headphones on their heads.

"Don't be nervous, kids. Even if thousands of people will be listening to you live, don't let it put you off."

He and a radio technician did voice checks on them, then twisted a few knobs, turned a few dials.

Laura glanced nervously around. She felt like they were sitting in a glass box with cotton wool in her ears. She could see right through to all the other studios, as well as the reception, where their friends waved and put their thumbs up. She could see all the technicians going about their normal jobs. Everything so strangely silent.

"The show is broadcast all through the building too," the presenter explained. "So your friends will be able to hear over the speakers. Now don't be nervous, we're going on air."

Butterflies began fluttering in Laura's stomach. And as the presenter played a musical jingle and went into his well-rehearsed patter, Laura pulled a terrified face at Gary.

"I'm scared!" she mimed silently at him.

Gary squeezed her hand, miming back. "Me too. But we have to do this – for Matty and for the animals … all of them."

The presenter turned down the music and introduced his first guests. Out in the reception area, their friends silently cheered through the sound-proof glass.

The presenter, still chatting, looked directly at them. *Ready?* his expression said.

Laura and Gary nodded.

"So to all of you listeners out there," the presenter continued, "I'll hand you over to our two young newsreaders who, they tell me, have something very important to say. Let's find out what it is…"

"Er… Good morn … afternoon, I mean," Laura mumbled into the microphone, turning crimson, feeling sick. The smile twitched on the presenter's face. She was going to mess this up. She couldn't do it. All those thousands of people listening to her...

Panic-stricken, she looked at Gary.

For the animals he mimed.

Pictures flashed through her head. All those animals killed for sport ... rhinos killed for their horns ... the white wolf's family...

The Colonel had caused so much pain. Now what was to become of the animals at the rare breeds park? With no one to pay for their upkeep, would they have to die too?

Laura glanced at her friends through the glass. Everyone seemed to be holding their breath.

For the animals, she told herself as she felt courage surge through her. For the ones that had died – and especially for the ones that could be saved!

Taking a deep breath, she spoke clearly into the microphone...

Chapter 24

Talking calmly and accurately, Laura and Gary re-told the whole story between them – taking it in turns naturally to speak, as if it had been rehearsed.

And if they thought it was quiet in the studio, outside you could have heard a pin drop!

Everyone – technicians, producers, visitors, secretaries – all had stopped what they were doing, to listen to the story being unravelled over the air.

Finally Gary left it to Laura to sum it all up.

"...so now there's no one to pay for the upkeep of the animals at Cottesbrook Rare Breeds Park. They need our help. Is there anyone..." she implored, "anyone at all who can give them some help ... before it's too late?"

She sank back in her chair, suddenly exhausted. Only then did they notice all the faces pressed up against the big studio windows. Instantaneously they all started clapping.

The presenter put a disc on to the turntable and smiled at them. "Excellent," he nodded approvingly. "Just excellent."

Almost instantly activity erupted beyond the studio windows.

Telephones started ringing. Although they couldn't be heard, people started dashing about to answer them. Someone, with the receiver to his ear waved frantically at them. His thumb went up!

"Looks like you've got someone interested," the presenter remarked with a wink.

A moment later, it was thumbs up from someone else on the phone. Then another and another. Someone dashed into the studio and handed the presenter a written message.

He read it. "Telephone lines jammed with

offers of help! Tell listeners we are setting up a hot line. Give them this number…"

Laura and Gary practically jumped for joy.

"Yes!" Gary cried, punching the air.

Laura felt so happy she could have burst.

They walked out of the studio to cheers and applause. One of the producers patted them on the back. "Good work, kids. And you, young lady, come back in a few years' time and there'll be a news reporter's job waiting for you!"

Outside there were more surprises — reporters and cameramen from the local news-papers, all wanting to hear the story again for themselves and their readers. And to photo-graph the youngsters who had uncovered the illegal business going on right here in their own town.

It seemed an age until Laura, Gary and Bethan were finally left alone.

Then Gary suddenly sprinted off.

"Gary! Where are you going?"

Still running, he shouted back. "Kess! I forgot all about Kess…" He shook his head miserably. "With everything going on, I forgot about her… How could I do that?"

"Come on," Laura said to Bethan. "Let's try and catch him up."

Hindered by snow, ice and slush, Gary could run no faster than the girls. They all arrived at the vet's surgery together.

Gary dashed in.

The vet was just showing his last patient out. "Ah, Gary…" he began but Gary pushed past him.

"I need to see Kess," he said. "She's all right, isn't she? I haven't had time to think about her … and I've got this awful feeling…"

"There has been a change…" the vet began.

"I knew it!" Gary wailed, dashing through to the recovery room. Laura and Bethan followed.

The room was empty.

Kess's bed had been scrubbed clean.

"She's died!"

Chapter 25

"No, she hasn't died!" the vet said sternly, turning Gary in the direction of the back door. "And if you'd just like to take a look out there, you'll see the change in her I was referring to."

They all went outside. It had started to snow again, soft light flakes drifting silently down.

For a moment all they could see was the small back yard, which backed on to a piece of wild open land. Rough and hilly with bramble bushes and a tree or two.

"I don't understand…" Gary murmured.

Then suddenly they heard something. That familiar high-pitched collie bark.

Kess's bark!

She came hobbling over the hill, one leg in plaster, but her beautiful golden fur gleaming in the afternoon sunlight. Her slim, sleek head was held high as she barked at the snow-flakes and tried to catch them on her tongue.

"Kess!" Gary cried, leaping the small wooden yard gate to race towards his dog.

Kess saw him and practically pulled Rachel off her feet to get off her lead and get to him.

Gary skidded on to his knees as Kess bounded on top of him, licking his face, her tail wagging like crazy. So excited and happy to be together again out in the fresh air.

Laura and Bethan raced towards them.

"Kess! You're better!" Laura cried, burying her face in her fur. "Thank goodness!"

"The vet says you can take her home," Rachel told Gary, happily.

"I can? When?" Gary asked urgently.

"Can't think of a better time than now, can you?" the vet added, strolling over to join them.

"Honestly? Oh! That's brilliant! Thanks! Thanks a million!"

"You're the ones who need thanking," the vet remarked as he scratched Kess behind the ears. "Showing that Colonel Cartwright-Holmes up for what he really is."

"You heard then?" Laura asked.

"The whole town did," said the vet. "And you don't need to worry about the park not being looked after. I have a lot of connections in the animal world myself. Although I heard over the radio the tremendous response you got. It's going to be fine, just fine."

"I can't believe it," Bethan exclaimed happily. "Isn't it all so wonderful!"

But Laura looked anxiously at the vet. "Do you think Matty will be allowed to keep his wolf? It's really not fierce. It's just like a big pet dog."

The vet smiled reassuringly. "I imagine there'll be one or two people to convince. But yes, Matty won't be parted from his wolf again. That's a promise."

"Brilliant!" Laura beamed. "The rare breeds park is going to be all right, Matty has his wolf back, and best of all, Gary has Kess back."

And as if Kess was agreeing whole-heartedly, she raised her sleek head, barked that distinctive bark of hers and gave Gary a big sloppy lick.

Everyone laughed and made a huge fuss of Kess.

"Animals," Laura sighed happily. "Don't you just love them!"